UP FROM THE DEPTHS . . .

The smoke rose up, spinning, spinning like a cyclone, and a sour stench filled the air. Corky gasped as the sickening odor swept over her.

She grabbed on to Kimmy and watched in horror as the black smoke whirled up.

The ice blistered and burned. The smoke spewed up, thicker, faster, swirling up over the shivering trees, up to the clouds.

"What have we done?" Corky cried, clinging to Kimmy.

"The evil!" Kimmy wailed.

"We brought the evil to life!" Corky realized. "We've *unleashed* it!"

Books by R. L. Stine

Available from ARCHWAY Paperbacks

FEAR STREET®
SUPER CHILLER
R·L·STINE

CHEERLEADERS
The New Evil

A Parachute Press Book

AN ARCHWAY PAPERBACK
Published by POCKET BOOKS
New York London Toronto Sydney Tokyo Singapore

This book is a work of fiction. Names, characters, places and incidents are products of the author's imagination or are used fictitiously. Any resemblance to actual events or locales or persons, living or dead, is entirely coincidental.

AN ARCHWAY PAPERBACK *Original*

An Archway Paperback published by
POCKET BOOKS, a division of Simon & Schuster Inc.
1230 Avenue of the Americas, New York, NY 10020

ISBN: 0-671-86835-7

First Archway Paperback printing December 1994

10 9 8 7 6 5 4 3 2 1

FEAR STREET is a registered trademark of Parachute Press, Inc.

AN ARCHWAY PAPERBACK and colophon are registered trademarks of Simon & Schuster Inc.

Cover art by David Jarvis

Printed in the U.S.A.

IL 7+

PART ONE

PARTY TIME

Chapter 1

THE CRASH DUMMY

HOOP—there it is!
HOOP—there it is!
TWOOOOOOOOO points!

Corky Corcoran laughed and clapped her hands. "Let's do it again!" she called to her two friends, Kimmy Bass and Hannah Miles, who had taken off running.

The three cheerleaders stopped in the middle of the empty student parking lot, a few feet from Kimmy's snow-covered car. Kimmy tossed a wet snowball at Hannah. Laughing, Hannah ducked and the snowball exploded against the car trunk.

3

Putting their arms around one another's shoulders, they enthusiastically repeated the cheer they'd been practicing in the gym.

> HOOP—there it is!
> HOOP—there it is!
> TWOOOOOOOOO points!

Hannah pulled free and performed a perfect cartwheel, her red wool scarf flying up behind her.

"Show-off!" Kimmy cried, her round cheeks even pinker than usual.

Hannah laughed and tossed a handful of snow back in Kimmy's direction. Then the three girls burst into the other cheer they'd worked out that afternoon.

> Where are we putting it?
> IN YOUR FACE!
> Where are we keeping it?
> IN YOUR FACE!
> Slam it, Tigers! Slam it!

The girls jumped up and down in the long, empty parking lot. Behind them the wind whipped around the brick school building, sending sprays of snow cascading off the window ledges.

Corky waved to Debra Kern and Heather Diehl, two other cheerleaders. They had just emerged from the gym and were hurrying through the snow toward Heather's car at the far end of the lot. "See you guys tomorrow!" Corky called.

The gusting wind carried away Debra's reply.

Corky pulled her hood over her blond hair and turned back to Kimmy and Hannah. "We've been cheering since school let out. Why are we standing out here doing more?" she cried.

"To keep warm?" Hannah suggested.

Kimmy shivered. She pulled a red and white wool ski cap on over her crimped black hair. "The car will be warmer," she suggested, slapping her gloves together. "If I can start her up."

Heading to the blue Camry, Corky slipped on a patch of ice. Kimmy caught her before she could fall. "Careful," she warned Corky. "Don't break your leg until *after* the Holiday Tournament."

"I'll try not to," Corky replied dryly. As Kimmy brushed snow off the windshield with her gloves, Corky gazed up at the sky. Dark as night. It had been snowing on and off for three days, and the heavy, low clouds appeared to be ready to deliver more.

Hannah slid into the passenger seat. Corky tossed her bag in first, then climbed into the back. She shut the door quickly. "It's colder in the car!" she declared, her breath steaming the window.

"The heater will warm things up," Kimmy said, sliding behind the wheel. It took her several tries to get the key in the ignition with her gloves on.

Kimmy let out a cheer as the car started right up. The tires crunched over the snow as she drove slowly past Shadyside High onto Park Drive.

Hannah reached out and clicked on the radio. "I *love* this song!" she cried, cranking up the volume. She pulled off her white wool cap and shook out her straight, black hair.

"Put on your seat belt," Kimmy told Hannah.

"No need," Hannah replied, bobbing in time to the music. "It's only a ten-minute drive to my house."

"But the streets are really slippery," Kimmy insisted, leaning over the wheel to see better through the icy windshield. "Haven't you seen the commercials on TV with those test dummies crashing through the windshield?"

Hannah laughed gleefully. "I *love* those guys!" she shouted over the music. "Kimmy, you're such a worrier."

"Whatever," Kimmy muttered, and concentrated on her driving.

Her hands shoved into her coat pockets, Corky settled back against the seat. Out the window, snow-covered houses and yards slid past, all white and gray, as if someone had drained away all the color.

Maybe we'll have a white Christmas, Corky thought.

Kimmy's voice broke into her thoughts. "Wasn't it a great practice? I think we're all really together. Finally."

"The new cheers are great," Hannah agreed. "If Naomi hadn't lost her contact lens—*again!*—we could have worked out the ending to the pyramid too."

"Hey, don't get on Naomi's case," Corky cut in. Naomi Klein was the new cheerleader on the squad, replacing Ronnie Mitchell, who'd switched to a different school. Naomi was really smart and talented, with a lot of good ideas.

Corky pictured Naomi. She was pretty and enthusiastic, with long, carrot-colored hair that flew around when she cheered. A trained gymnast, Naomi brought a lot of new energy and expertise to the squad.

"Well, does she have to lose her contact every day?" Hannah complained. "I mean, can't she glue it in or something?"

Kimmy laughed.

Hannah is jealous of Naomi, Corky realized. Last year, Hannah was the exciting new star. Now Naomi had taken her place.

"Naomi's ideas for the fire baton routine were excellent," Kimmy commented, carefully steering the car out of a little skid. "I think Ms. Closter resents Naomi."

Ms. Closter was the new cheerleader coach. She replaced Miss Green, who had moved away.

"Huh? Why would Ms. Closter resent Naomi?" Corky asked, tracing a pattern over the fogged window.

"Because Naomi's routines are better than hers," Kimmy replied.

Hannah leaned forward to crank up the volume on the radio. "This song is so incredible!" she declared. "Have you heard the unplugged version? It's great too!"

Through the haze on the windshield, Corky saw the red glare of a traffic light. Kimmy eased the car to a stop, turning the wheel as the tires started to slide into the left lane. "Why don't they salt these streets?" she complained over the booming music.

"Are you seeing Alex after the basketball game Friday night?" Hannah asked Corky, turning to the backseat.

Corky nodded. "Yeah. I guess."

"Dumb question," Kimmy muttered. "What *else* would she be doing?"

Corky felt her face grow hot and knew she was blushing. She'd been going with Alex for a month, but she still felt uncomfortable talking about him, even with her best friends.

It's not like Alex and I have any agreement, Corky thought wistfully. We just sort of end up getting together most weekends.

Alex was one of the most popular guys at Shadyside High. *Too* popular, Corky told herself. On Saturday, she had seen him at the mall kidding around with Deena Martinson. The week before Kimmy had reported seeing Alex's car parked in Janie Simpson's driveway.

"I was helping her with her English," Alex had explained when Corky confronted him later in her front yard. He had grinned at her, his blue eyes lighting up. "Jealous?"

"No way!" Corky had insisted, giving him a hard, playful shove that sent him sprawling in the snow.

The next moment the two were wrestling in the snow, laughing and shouting happily.

It was hard to stay angry at Alex, Corky realized. He was so good-looking, with that great blond hair and those dark blue eyes that crinkled up when he smiled. *And* he was a real brain. *And* he was the center on the basketball team. A shoo-in for all-state this season. And . . . and . . .

"Hey!" Kimmy's shout interrupted Corky's daydreams about Alex. The car skidded hard, then slid to a stop at the curb as a large van roared past.

"Did you see how fast that guy was going?" Kimmy complained, watching the van in the rearview mirror. "Is he crazy or what? He was sliding all over the street!" The tires spun as she started the car up again.

"Maybe you should drop me at Corky's," Hannah shouted after a minute. "I just remembered. My parents are at some meeting. No one will be home." She turned back to Corky. "What's your mom serving for dinner tonight?"

Corky laughed. "I don't know. But why don't you invite yourself over?"

"Okay. Thanks," Hannah replied, turning back to the front.

"So I'm driving to your house?" Kimmy called back to Corky. "Hey, I really can't hear a thing. Hannah, could you turn it down a little?"

"What? I can't hear you. The music is too loud!" Hannah joked.

As Hannah leaned forward to turn down the radio, Kimmy let out a frightened cry.

The car swerved.

"Kimmy—what *is* it?" she managed to call out.

The car bolted forward.

"The brakes!" Kimmy squealed.

9

The car went into a spin. Corky screamed.

The wide tree trunk came up so quickly, covering the windshield in darkness.

A hard jolt tossed Corky against the seat, then forward, hard.

It all happened in an instant. The crunch of metal jarred her ears.

Corky saw Hannah fly forward.

Her head hit the windshield with a sickening *crack*.

The glass shattered and broke into tiny pellets. The car bounced.

Corky heard Kimmy gasp as she was thrown against the steering wheel. Then Kimmy's sharp whisper: "No—no—no . . ."

Corky checked on Hannah. Hannah's body. Through the shattered windshield. Her legs dangling down over the dashboard. The top of her body sprawled over the car hood.

Chapter 2

THE EVIL IS BACK

"The evil is back," Kimmy murmured, shutting her eyes.

Corky swallowed hard. "Kimmy—no!" she whispered.

Two doctors in green surgical scrubs hurried past, their faces yellow under the harsh fluorescent lights.

The waiting room at Shadyside General blazed with heat, but Corky hadn't removed her down jacket. She sat huddled beside Kimmy on a vinyl couch, tensing every time a doctor or nurse passed, waiting for news about Hannah.

"I could feel it in the car," Kimmy murmured, her face pale, her chin trembling. "I could feel the evil." She shuddered.

11

"Kimmy—stop it," Corky pleaded. She placed a hand on the sleeve of Kimmy's sweater. "Your brakes gave out. That's all."

"It was the evil!" Kimmy wailed.

An old man rolled slowly past, bent over in a wheelchair. He gazed over at Kimmy, then continued wheeling himself down a long corridor.

"Kimmy, the brakes froze. That's all," Corky insisted firmly. "It's not your fault. It's not anyone's fault. We just have to pray that Hannah's going to be okay."

Kimmy lowered her eyes to the floor. Her crimped black hair had fallen over her forehead, but she made no attempt to brush it away. She clutched her chest where she had hit the steering wheel. But the doctor told her she had no broken ribs.

"The evil—" she whispered.

"The evil is gone," Corky said sharply. "We drowned it. In the river—remember? It's under the ice now. Buried deep in the frozen river."

Kimmy didn't reply.

"You can't blame the evil spirit every time something bad happens," Corky told her friend. "You have to forget about it. Sometimes bad things happen. They can't be helped."

Corky's words rang hollow in her own ears. She felt the same way that Kimmy did. Whenever anything went wrong, Corky found herself wondering if the evil had returned.

She couldn't forget it. She remembered it every day of her life.

She remembered another Shadyside cheerleader, Jennifer Daly, who had died when the cheerleaders' bus had crashed into the Fear Street Cemetery. An evil spirit awakened from its resting place in a hundred-year-old grave. The evil swarmed into Jennifer, took possession of her body, and brought her back to life.

The spirit used Jennifer's body to perform its evil. It murdered Corky's sister Bobbi. And it murdered others.

After a terrifying struggle, Corky thought she had defeated the evil. Jennifer was buried. But the evil was still loose. It moved on to Kimmy. Then to Corky. It forced them to carry out its vicious acts of terror.

Finally, I drowned it, Corky remembered with a shudder. I freed myself. I drowned the evil. That was the only way to defeat it.

But even though I forced it from my body, I couldn't get rid of the memories of it. They stayed with me. The *fear* stayed with me.

The fear that it might return. The fear that it might take over my mind again, use me again, force me to become evil again.

Corky turned back to Kimmy. Kimmy was hugging her coat tightly. Her eyes watered with tears. Her round cheeks were crimson.

"Kimmy—Hannah will be okay," Corky assured her. "You just have to keep saying that. Her parents are upstairs with her. They'll come down any minute and tell us she's going to be okay."

Clutching her coat still tighter, Kimmy stared straight ahead. She didn't seem to hear Corky.

I'm glad Kimmy's parents are on their way, Corky thought, patting her friend's arm. I think maybe Kimmy is in shock or something.

"Debra thinks the evil will come back," Kimmy murmured, a single teardrop rolling slowly down one cheek.

Debra Kern was the only other girl who knew the whole story of the ancient evil.

"Debra has always been weird," Corky replied sharply. "A few days after I met her, I found her trying to cast a sleep spell on her dog."

Kimmy didn't smile. "Debra knows a lot about a lot of weird stuff," she said in a flat, dead voice.

"You've been spending too much time with Debra," Corky told her friend. "Reading those dusty old books of hers, studying all that strange stuff. Just because Debra is into that stuff again doesn't mean—"

"I'm really interested in it too," Kimmy confessed. "After what happened to us . . ." Her voice trailed off.

Corky glanced up as Hannah's parents approached them. Mrs. Miles had Hannah's dark hair and dark eyes. She clung tightly to her husband's arm. Mr. Miles was short and chubby. His gray overcoat came down nearly to the floor. His eyes were red-rimmed and watery.

As they stepped into the waiting room, Corky jumped to her feet and hurried over to them. "How is Hannah?" she cried. "Is she going to be okay?"

Mrs. Miles let out a loud sob.

Chapter 3

SURPRISE AT THE RIVER

> Down the floor,
> Shoot two more!
> Down the floor,
> Shoot two more!
> Go, TIGERS!

Corky leapt into the spread eagle that finished the cheer. She came down awkwardly and twisted her ankle.

Down the row, she watched Debra start her spread eagle late, change her mind midair, and drop back to the ground without completing it.

After the accident, cheerleader practices had been canceled. Now, two days later, everyone was feeling

15

rusty, Corky, who had just been elected co-captain, realized.

Ms. Closter blew her whistle, a shrill note of disapproval. "Whoa! Just whoa!" she called, raising both hands as she stepped toward the cheerleaders.

The coach was a short, pencil-thin woman of thirty or thirty-five, Corky guessed. She always wore a long white T-shirt that came nearly to her knees over gray leggings. She had a plain, slender face with gray eyes that were somehow always unhappy. She wore a dark blue and gold Notre Dame cap backward over her short brown hair.

"You're cheering like the walking wounded today," she scolded, tossing her whistle back over her shoulder.

"Let's try it again!" Kimmy shouted. Her round cheeks were bright pink. She had a line of sweat on her top lip even though they had barely begun to practice. "Let's really shout!"

As co-captain with Corky, Kimmy saw it as her job to cheer the others on when their energy was low. That day they all were like lumps in their gray sweats and T-shirts. No energy at all.

"Whoa," Ms. Closter repeated. Her favorite phrase. "One word, girls." She cleared her throat. "It's our first practice without Hannah, and we all miss her—right? We all feel bad that she's in the hospital."

"I talked to her mother this morning before school," Corky reported.

"And what did she say?" Ms. Closter asked, resting

16

her hands on her slender waist. "How is Hannah doing?"

"She—she's stable," Corky replied, glancing at Kimmy. And then she added, "Whatever that means."

Ms. Closter nodded solemnly. "I hope that means they've stopped the internal bleeding."

Corky shrugged. "The doctor just said she was stable. Her mother said Hannah's face was really cut up. She needed a lot of stitches. And she broke her collarbone. But she should come through it all okay."

Debra let out a low sigh. Naomi and Heather shook their heads.

"It could have been worse," Ms. Closter murmured, fiddling with the string that held her whistle. "She could've broken her neck. In a way, Hannah was lucky."

"Yeah. Real lucky," Debra muttered, rolling her eyes.

"I know this sounds a little cold," Kimmy said, pushing back her dark bangs. "But we have to think about the Holiday Tournament. What are we going to do about replacing Hannah?"

Ms. Closter knitted her brow. "We'll hold tryouts Monday after school. If you know anyone who's interested—"

"But the tournament's just two weeks away!" Heather protested. "How will the new person learn the routines?"

"Practice," Ms. Closter replied, turning her cap

around to the front. "A lot of practice." She motioned with both hands. "Okay, everyone. Line up. Spread eagles. Again. This time with some energy. Think light. *Light*. You're light as feathers."

Naomi sneezed loudly. She rubbed her nose. "I'm allergic to feathers!" she cried.

The girls all laughed. Corky forced a laugh too. But her mind wasn't on practice. She was thinking only about Hannah.

Ms. Closter said Hannah was lucky, Corky thought fretfully. I don't think Hannah would agree.

And if Kimmy is right, if the evil has returned, then *none* of us are lucky.

Kimmy *can't* be right, though, Corky decided.

She took her place at the end of the line. Shaking her head hard, she tried to chase away all scary thoughts.

Across the gym, the door to the boys' locker room swung open. The boys' basketball team came jogging out and began dribbling in wide circles.

Corky waved to Alex, but he didn't see her. He and his best friend, Jay Landers, started passing a basketball rapidly back and forth.

"Same cheer!" Ms. Closter instructed. "Really shout. Make the backboards shatter!"

Ms. Closter's words made Corky gasp. She saw the broken windshield. Hannah's body sprawled over the hood.

The cheer started. Corky came in a beat late. She struggled to catch up.

> Down the floor,
> Shoot two more!
> Down the floor,
> Shoot two more!
> Go, TIGERS!

Up into her spread eagle now. Her eyes on Alex. Why doesn't he turn around? Corky wondered. Why doesn't he watch?

A good jump. Her legs straight out. Down now. Into a split.

Yes! Looking good!

Everyone up at the same time. Jump. Clap. Cheer. And run off.

"Better!" Ms. Closter shouted over the drumbeat of dribbling basketballs. "A lot better. Let's try it again. Debra, that was your best jump yet. Come on. Line up."

"Uh—I've got a leg cramp," Corky called to the coach. "Be right back. I need to walk it off."

She pretended to limp as she made her way to the far side of the gym. "Hey—Alex!" she called.

Jay saw her first. Tucking the basketball under his arm, he flashed her a smile and waved. "Corky— looking good!"

Corky liked Jay. A lot of girls thought he was goofy, mainly because he was always grinning his toothy grin. And always cracking dumb jokes and giggling uproariously at them. Or deliberately walking into a wall for a cheap laugh.

With his long, crooked nose, tiny brown eyes, and short, spiky white-blond hair, Jay looked like a very tall chicken. But Corky thought he was fun. She always defended him when other girls talked about what a geek he was.

"Hey, Alex!" she called.

Alex finally noticed her. He came dribbling over. Jay deliberately bounced his ball into Alex's foot. Alex casually kicked Jay's ball away. "What's up, Cork?"

"Do you have your car?" Corky asked. She pushed a wave of blond hair off her forehead.

He nodded. "Yeah. You need a lift home?"

Corky hesitated. "Can we take a short ride? After practice?"

Alex narrowed his blue eyes in confusion. "A ride? I promised my mom I'd be home by dinnertime."

"Just to the river and back," Corky told him.

"Don't drive with Alex," Jay broke in, grinning. "He gets carsick."

"Hey, Landers!" Alex protested. "I get sick only when I look at your face. It's like someone drove over it!"

Jay shoved Alex out of the way. *"I'll* take you to the river, Corky," he offered, spinning the ball on one finger.

"You have a car?" Corky asked.

"No. But so what?" Jay opened his mouth in a high-pitched laugh.

Alex rolled his eyes. "Why do you want to drive to the river?"

Corky didn't get a chance to answer. She heard Ms.

Closter's whistle. "Corky—no time-outs!" the coach called. "We're waiting for you."

"Okay. Meet me after practice," Alex agreed. He turned, dribbled across the floor, stopped at the three-point circle, and sent the ball flying. It swished through—all net.

Alex turned back to Corky and grinned, the cute, boyish grin that always made Corky want to hug him.

"Lucky shot!" Corky heard Jay declare as she hurried back to practice.

"How was practice?" Corky asked Alex, lowering herself into the passenger seat of his father's white Sable and pulling the door shut.

"Better than yours," Alex replied. "I heard Ms. Closter yelling at you guys." He shook his head.

He's so great looking, Corky thought. She liked the way his blond hair, wild and unbrushed as always, fell over his forehead. And she liked the tiny dimple that appeared in his right cheek when he smiled.

"We weren't into it today," Corky said quietly.

Alex pushed back the hood of his parka, then started the car. Corky gazed up at the late afternoon sky. A pale moon already poked over the winter-bare trees. It gets dark so early in December, she thought.

The charcoal-gray sky matched her mood. She slumped in the seat, raising her knees to the glove compartment as Alex pulled out onto Park Drive. Some of the snow had melted. But there were still patches of ice on the street.

"Did you see me reject Gary Brandt's layup?" Alex

asked gleefully. "His mouth dropped open so wide, he nearly swallowed the ball!" He laughed. "I can't wait for the tournament. I think we're going to kick some butt!"

The car slid as Alex turned sharply onto River Road. Corky adjusted the seat belt over the front of her blue down jacket. They rolled past three little kids having a frantic snowball fight in a wide front yard. "Hey—no ice balls!" Corky heard one of them yell.

"What was that big crowd around Jay?" Corky asked. "I saw you running over to him."

"Gary and Jay collided. Jay thought he broke his nose!" Alex declared, snickering.

"Huh?" Corky lowered her legs and sat up. "Was he okay?"

"With *his* nose, who could tell?" Alex joked.

"He's supposed to be your best friend," Corky scolded playfully.

"Does that mean I have to like his nose?" Alex shot back.

They both laughed. Corky leaned closer to Alex.

The road curved up along the Conononka River, past dark trees, shivering in a brisk wind. Through the trees, Corky glimpsed a solid blanket of white.

"The river is completely frozen over," she murmured, feeling a little relieved.

"Why'd you want to come up here?" Alex demanded, pumping the brake pedal as the car started to spin at a curve.

"Slow down!" Corky instructed. "If we go over the side—"

Alex finished the sentence for her. "We'll be dead— and my dad will go ballistic because I bent up his new car."

The tires crunched over the hard snow. He eased the car to a stop at the side of the road before they made it all the way to the top of the overlook. Swaying tree branches cracked above them.

Alex shifted the car into park and left the engine running. He rubbed his hands together, warming them in front of the heater vent. "So why'd you want to come up here?" he repeated, a smile crossing his face.

He leaned toward her, reached out, and pulled her close. Before Corky could resist, he was kissing her.

His nose felt cold, but his lips were warm. Corky snuggled against him, returning the kiss.

She ended it by gently pushing him back. "That *isn't* why I wanted to drive up here," she said softly.

He pursed his lips into an exaggerated pout. "You sure?" He reached for her again as Corky pushed open her door. And climbed out of the car.

The sudden cold surprised her, made her gasp. A gust of wind held the car door open. She struggled to close it.

Gripping the car keys in one hand, Alex came around the front of the car to join her. "If you're thinking about a swim, forget it!" he joked, shivering.

She pulled the two sides of his parka together. "Why don't you zip up?" she asked.

He shrugged. "Because I'm macho."

"No. Because you're stupid," she corrected him.

23

He did his pout again.

She laughed and led the way through the trees, her Doc Martens crunching over the hard snow. The cold wind swirled off the river, making the trees creak and bend.

Alex hurried to catch up with her. He pulled the parka hood over his head and then took her hand. "N-nice day for a w-walk," he said, shivering some more.

"I just have to see the river," Corky told him. "It's hard to explain."

"Well, here it is," Alex announced as they came out of the trees. "It looks like an ice rink." He tugged her arm. "Can we go back now?"

"In one second," she replied. The wind made her eyes water. She shielded them with a gloved hand and squinted out at the frozen river.

A solid sheet of ice from shore to shore.

The whipping wind sent sprays of snow up off the frozen surface.

Yes, it's totally iced over, Corky saw, beginning to feel a little better. The evil has to be buried still down where I left it. Nothing could escape that solid block of ice.

Nothing. Not even the evil.

And then Corky's eyes settled on something and she let out a low, startled cry.

And pointed in horror.

She gripped the sleeve of Alex's parka. "What's *that?*" Corky cried.

Chapter 4

NIGHT VISITOR

*A*lex's eyes darted over the ice. "What's your problem?" he asked, sliding an arm around her shoulders.

"What *is* that?" Corky repeated shrilly. The wind swirled wet snow in her face. She squinted, trying to see clearly in the fading light.

"You mean that hole in the ice?" Alex asked, bewildered. "It's an ice-fishing hole."

Corky took a step toward it, then stopped. The moon cast long tree shadows over the frozen river. The white ice glowed eerily.

Squinting hard, Corky could make out white steam, ghostlike against the dark sky, billowing up from the hole.

"It—it's escaping," Corky murmured, unable to hold in her horror.

"Huh?" Alex gaped at her, trying to figure out what had frightened her. "Corky? What's wrong?"

She pointed again, her hand trembling.

"The steam?" he asked, confused. "That's steam shooting up from the hole. It's because the water below the ice is warmer than the air above the ice."

No, Corky thought, gripping Alex's sleeve. No, it isn't steam.

But how can I tell Alex what it really is? How can I tell him that it is the evil swirling up to find a victim to inhabit?

I can't.

The white vapor continued to rise up against the dark sky, twisting in the gusting wind. "Alex, let's get out of here," Corky pleaded.

The cracks resembled a ladder, a very tall ladder tilting off into the distance. Lying on her back in bed, Corky gazed up at the ceiling, unable to sleep.

She had tried calling Kimmy after dinner, but got the answering machine. Then she tried Debra. But her father answered, sounding confused. He said he didn't know where Debra or her mother had gone.

Finally Corky telephoned the hospital to speak to Hannah. But a nurse told her Hannah was resting and couldn't be disturbed.

Feeling shaky and alone, Corky had struggled to concentrate on her homework. Then she went to bed early, hoping to fall asleep and escape her frightening thoughts.

But she found no escape.

Wide awake, she stared up at the spidery cracks in the ceiling, thinking about Hannah, about the accident, about the evil, about her sister Bobbi, about the steam swirling up so eerily from the hole in the frozen river.

The ceiling cracks suddenly appeared to move.

Corky's eyes grew wide. She lifted her head from the pillow, staring hard.

The cracks shimmered. But they weren't moving.

Then Corky saw the steam floating across her ceiling.

A fine white mist moving silently as a cloud.

Silent as death, Corky thought.

The steam filled the top of her room, then started to curl down.

I've got to get out of here! Corky told herself, panic choking her throat, cutting off her breathing. Why can't I move?

Why?

She lay frozen in place, gazing up in cold horror as the steamy blanket lowered itself on top of her.

And as it swept over the bed, over her body, descending over her face, she began to feel the anger build inside her.

Felt the anger burn her chest.

Felt the angry flames shoot out through her body.
Until the anger turned to rage.

And she opened her mouth in a roar of hate.

I am a *monster* again! she told herself.

I am back, back for good.

Chapter 5

DARKNESS AT DEBRA'S

"Corky!"

"Corky!"

Voices called to her, tried to get through the billowing fog. Hot hands grabbed her roughly. Shook her.

"Corky!"

"Corky—please!"

She opened her eyes to find her parents beside her bed. Her mother held her by the shoulders. Her father leaned close, calling her name.

"Another nightmare!" Mrs. Corcoran murmured, loosening her grip but still holding on. "Corky—are you awake now?"

"That was a bad one," Corky's dad said. "You haven't screamed like that in a long time."

"Just a dream," Corky managed to whisper, gazing up at her worried parents.

No drifting steam in her room. No evil cloud of vapor over her bed. No spirit lowering itself into her mind.

Of course. It was only a dream.

Wasn't it?

She had the same nightmare at least once a month. Ever since the evil had inhabited her body, had used her for its plots.

In her sleep she had felt the anger return, felt the anger flame until it burst out of her in a howl of rage.

Just a dream. Of course, just a dream.

So why did it seem different this time?

Why did it seem so much more real?

Alex slammed the table with both hands. "It was all my fault!" he cried angrily. "I blew it! I totally blew it!"

"Hey, superstar—" Jay reached across the table and playfully punched Alex's jaw. "No one is blaming you."

"Why not?" Alex demanded. "I let the guy shoot. I let the ball go in. I lost the game for us—didn't I?"

"Nice weather we're having," Corky commented dryly. She wondered if she should just get up and leave. She could see that Alex and Jay were going to replay the basketball game for the rest of Friday night.

How dreary.

Corky felt the same combination of excitement and

exhaustion she felt after every game. Her throat was scratchy from cheering. Her leg muscles ached. But her heart was still racing. And she wanted to cheer more or dance until she dropped.

They were squeezed into a booth in the back of Pete's Pizza at the mall. Corky sat beside Jay. Alex slumped across the table from them.

A large pepperoni pizza sat in the middle of the white Formica table. So far, Corky was the only one who had taken a slice.

"I jumped too soon, that's all," Alex said glumly, resting his chin in his hands. "Otherwise, I would've blocked the shot."

"Give me a break, Alex. He faked you out of your Nikes!" Jay shot back, letting out his high-pitched giggle. He had a Mighty Ducks cap pulled down over his short, spiky hair and looked goofier than ever.

"Are you trying to cheer me up or what?" Alex asked, scowling.

Jay pulled two round pieces of pepperoni off the pizza and covered his eyes with them. "Hey—do you think I need glasses?"

Corky laughed. At least Jay was trying to get over his disappointment. Alex continued to scowl and shake his head.

"So we lost in the last second," Jay continued, removing the pepperonis from his eyes and popping them into his mouth. "Think of it this way, Alex, we won the first forty-seven minutes and fifty-nine seconds of the game!"

Corky laughed. Jay can always make me laugh, she thought. Alex picked up a slice of pizza, then set it down again.

"The game doesn't even count!" Jay insisted. "We're still going to the tournament, man! The tournament is what counts. That's the top ten teams in the state! That's the real season!"

"Guess you're right," Alex replied. He shrugged. Then all at once Corky saw a smile cross his face. Alex's blue eyes lit up for the first time since they'd arrived.

He's finally cheering up! Corky told herself.

But then she realized that Alex wasn't smiling at her. His eyes were focused over her shoulder.

She turned—and immediately saw two girls she knew from Shadyside High in the next booth. Jade Smith and Deena Martinson. Deena was tossing back her blond hair and flashing Alex a smile.

"What's going on here?" Corky blurted out angrily, turning back to Alex.

His smile quickly faded. "Huh? What do you mean?" Bright red circles formed on his cheeks. "Oh. I was just saying hi to those girls. You know. Deena and Jade."

Corky eyed him suspiciously. Alex laughed. "What's your problem, Corky?"

She continued to glare at him and didn't reply.

"Let's talk about the game," Jay broke in, trying to cut the tension. "Didn't I look awesome tonight? Did you see me jump three feet for that slam dunk?"

"Too bad you didn't have the ball!" Alex replied, grinning.

"Too bad you hit your head on the backboard!" Corky added.

She joined in the laughter. But didn't feel like laughing. Alex had stopped smiling at Deena, but now he avoided Corky too.

Is something going on between them? Corky wondered.

Why do I suddenly have such a bad feeling about Alex?

About the tournament?

About everything?

She tried to call Kimmy on Sunday afternoon. She had to talk to *someone* about Alex. They had made plans to go to the movies on Saturday. But Alex called at the last minute with a lame excuse about how he had to stay home and watch his little sister.

His voice sounded so strange, Corky thought. Alex is such a bad liar. She pictured him hanging up the phone and running out to meet Deena. Feeling miserable, she spent Saturday night playing with her brother, Sean. He forced her to play game after game of Mortal Kombat. He beat her every game.

The phone rang three times at Kimmy's house. "Come on, Kimmy—be home!" Corky urged out loud. I haven't even had a chance to tell her about what I saw at the river, Corky thought, pressing the receiver to her ear. About the hole in the ice and the weird vapor rising out of it.

After the fifth ring, Mrs. Bass answered breathlessly. She told Corky that Kimmy had gone over to Debra's house.

Corky borrowed her mother's car and drove to Debra's house on Canyon Road. The heavy gray clouds had finally drifted away, revealing a shimmering blue sky. Bright sunlight made the snowy lawns sparkle like silver.

The light glared off Corky's windshield. But the sun brought no warmth. The temperature stayed at twenty. The streets remained icy and slick.

She recognized the car parked at the curb in front of Debra's house—the blue Corolla Kimmy must have borrowed from her father. Kimmy's car was still in the garage having its front end repaired and the shattered windshield replaced.

Corky pulled her car up Debra's driveway and peered out at the sprawling white-shingled house. The walk and front stoop had been shoveled, but drifts of snow rose up to the front windows. The windows were all frosted over.

Her Doc Martens sliding on the slick walk, Corky made her way to the front door and rang the bell. Kimmy and Debra are probably doing homework together, she realized. I should have brought my backpack.

No reply. She tried the bell again, but she couldn't hear it ring inside the house. It was probably broken.

So she knocked. "Hey, Debra—it's me!" she called. "Open up!"

Still no reply.

They must be in the back, she decided. She tried the door—and it opened.

"Where *are* you?" Corky called, stepping into the front hallway. "Hey—Debra? Kimmy? It's me!"

The entire house appeared dark.

And silent.

Corky peeked into the living room. "Hey—guys?" she called meekly.

The drapes were drawn over the windows, shutting out all sunlight. No lamps were lit. Corky stared into the darkness. "Debra?"

A flicker of pale light caught her eye across the large living room. It's in the den, Corky realized. She took a few hesitant steps toward the dim light.

Candlelight?

"Hey—Debra? Are you in there?"

No reply.

The flickering circle of light grew brighter as Corky approached the den. She stopped in the open doorway —and gasped.

"What's going on?" Corky cried in a shocked whisper.

Chapter 6

"COME FORWARD, SPIRIT"

Corky watched the light flicker across her friends' faces from the candles. Their eyes were staring unblinking into the flames. The room was dark, the drapes drawn.

Debra and Kimmy knelt on the den floor, candles arranged in a circle between them.

Debra held a long red candle in one hand and was slowly passing it over the circle of candles. A large book lay open on the floor in front of her.

Both girls' lips moved silently. As Corky cried out, they continued to stare into the flames, concentrating so hard, they didn't hear her.

Corky remained in the doorway, unwilling to step into the room. She didn't like Debra's strange chants.

Finally Kimmy raised her eyes. Her expression changed to surprise. "Corky—what are *you* doing here? How did you get in?"

Debra groaned and straightened up, raising her candle from the others. "You ruined it," she complained.

"What on earth are you doing?" Corky asked, taking a reluctant step closer.

Debra climbed to her feet. She stretched her arms above her head. "Did you ring? The doorbell is broken. It froze, I think."

"The door was open," Corky explained, staring down into the candlelight. "Kimmy's mom said she was here, so—"

Debra pushed past Corky. "Oh. There's the phone. Be right back. Then you can help us." She hurried out of the room.

"Help you do *what?*" Corky asked Kimmy.

Kimmy lowered herself to a sitting position. She wore an oversize wool sweater and black leggings. "Debra found an old chant we're trying," she explained casually.

She leaned back on her hands. The orange light danced over her face and black hair. Her eyes glowed as they studied Corky. "Did you go out with Alex last night?"

Corky lowered herself to her knees beside Kimmy. "No. He called and said he couldn't make it." She sighed. "He gave a really lame-o excuse."

Kimmy *tsk-tsked.*

"Wish I didn't like him so much," Corky confessed.

37

She bent to pull off her shoes. They were still cold from being outside.

"Okay. Let's try again," Debra said, returning to the den. "This is great. With three of us chanting, the power will be much stronger."

Corky reluctantly got down on the floor beside Kimmy. "But what are you chanting about?" she demanded. "What are you trying to do?"

"We're trying to make Alex appear in the den!" Kimmy joked. "With no clothes on."

Debra's cold blue eyes narrowed at Kimmy. "Come on. No jokes. The spirits won't take us seriously."

Debra lowered herself to her knees on the other side of the ring of candles. Then she leaned over the big book on the floor and studied it.

"It's a chant to summon a spirit," Kimmy explained, lowering her voice to a whisper. "Debra found it in a book we bought in a used-book shop."

Debra continued to study the old book.

"What spirit?" Corky asked, whispering. "The evil spirit?"

"No—of course not!" Kimmy replied, her eyes on Debra. "We want to call up a different spirit—a spirit to protect us."

"You mean—" Corky started.

Debra raised a hand to silence them. Her eyes caught the firelight as she gazed at Corky. "We're going to call up a spirit to protect us from the evil. In case the evil really has returned. We—"

"That's what I wanted to tell you," Corky interrupted. "I went to the river, where I drowned the evil. The river is frozen over."

"I know that," Debra replied sharply. "I've gone skating on it. Lots of kids have been skating there. It's been frozen for a few weeks."

"Well, I saw a hole in the ice," Corky reported breathlessly.

"Huh?" Kimmy cried out in surprise.

"A pretty big hole, perfectly round," Corky reported. "And there was smoke pouring up from it. Like thick, evil fog. Pouring up from under the ice."

"Probably just steam," Debra murmured thoughtfully.

"You really think the evil has escaped?" Kimmy asked. "Do you think Hannah's accident . . ." Her voice trailed off as her eyes grew wide with fear.

"*You* put the idea in my head," Corky told Kimmy. "When your brakes gave out and we crashed. Was it just an accident? Or was the evil back, looking for revenge?"

Corky sighed. "I've been obsessing about it ever since. I even dream about it."

"The evil can come back only if it inhabits someone living," Debra said softly. "And there were only the three of you in the car."

Corky shuddered. "It's not in me," she reported. "I—I feel pretty normal."

"Me too," Kimmy replied quickly.

A loud sound made all three of them jump. It took Corky a few seconds to realize it was just the crash of a metal garbage can, toppled by the wind.

"Let's summon a spirit," Debra urged, picking up a long red candle from beside her on the floor, holding it over a flame to light it. "If the evil is back, we will need a spirit on *our* side to fight it."

"How do you know this will work?" Corky demanded.

"It's a very old book," Debra replied. "The store owner didn't want to sell it to me. He said it might be dangerous."

"Probably just trying to raise the price of the book," Corky suggested.

"Maybe he was telling the truth," Debra replied solemnly. She motioned impatiently to Corky to move closer to the candles.

I really hate this, Corky thought. It frightens me too much.

But, following Kimmy's lead, she knelt and leaned over the ring of candles, so close she could feel the warmth. She listened to Debra's soft chant.

"Come forward, spirit," Debra murmured, moving her candle in a slow, steady circle. "Come forward, spirit, to do our bidding."

Corky leaned closer. The candlelight danced as Debra began to chant, in a low singsong, strange words in a language Corky had never heard. Reading from the book, Debra chanted the words over and over.

As she chanted, Debra raised her eyes to Corky and Kimmy. "Join in," she instructed.

Leaning over the candle flames, the three girls chanted in unison.

Corky stopped chanting when she heard the creaking footsteps. Soft but steady from the living room. She and Kimmy exchanged glances.

Debra motioned impatiently for them to keep chanting.

Their voices grew softer as the creaking footsteps approached.

Glancing up, Corky saw the pictures on the den wall begin to shake. A low rumble competed with the creaking footsteps. The walls appeared to tremble. China figures on a shelf shook and nearly toppled to the floor.

"It's working!" Debra whispered excitedly, her eyes flashing in the dancing firelight.

Corky felt her throat tighten, but pushed herself to keep chanting. Their voices suddenly sounded tiny over the roaring sound that swirled around them.

The walls shook. The floor began to vibrate.

The whole room is shaking! Corky realized, forcing herself to repeat the strange words.

The footsteps drew closer.

Corky raised her eyes to the doorway. She could hear someone approaching.

But there was no one there.

No one.

The walls trembled. The floor shook. A picture dropped off the wall and fell with a clatter.

"Who—who's there?" Corky cried out.

She felt a rush of cold air. A musty odor swept through the room.

And all the candles went out at once.

41

Chapter 7

ACCIDENT IN THE GYM

Corky struggled to breathe, the musty odor choking her. A heavy chill settled over the darkness.

Kimmy let out a gasp.

Corky blinked as a light flashed on. Debra had climbed to her feet and clicked on a table lamp. "Spirit—come forward!" Debra cried, her eyes searching the room.

Corky turned toward the doorway. No one there.

"Stop! Stop it!" Kimmy screamed, jumping to her feet. Her face was bright red. Her hair wild about her head. "Please stop it, Debra! I'm too scared!"

"The spirit has left," Debra replied calmly. "I could feel its presence. It was here in this room. But now it has gone."

42

"I don't believe this!" Corky cried, standing up. Her legs weak and rubbery. "We really called up a spirit!"

The room had stopped shaking. Only the damp chill remained.

Kimmy let out a sigh. "Sorry I screamed like that," she said, smoothing her hair down with both hands. "I—I just got so scared!"

"Me too," Corky confessed. She stared down at the ring of still-smoking candles. "I was terrified."

"Something was here in this room," Debra said with surprising calmness. "If we hadn't panicked, it would have stayed. It wouldn't have vanished. Gone back to wherever it lives."

"Put the book away!" Kimmy insisted. She picked up the big book, slammed it shut, and thrust it at Debra. "Hide it. The man in the bookstore was right. It's too dangerous."

"We have to try to forget about chanting and magic spells," Corky urged, starting to breathe normally again. "We have to try to put it all in the past. It's just too frightening. We have to try to lead normal lives."

A bitter laugh escaped Debra's throat. Her cold eyes locked on Corky's. "Normal? After all that's happened here?"

"Corky is right," Kimmy insisted heatedly. "Hide the book, Debra. We were only looking for trouble."

"Okay, okay." Debra rolled her eyes. "I'm outvoted. I'll put it up in my room. I'll save it for a rainy day."

Corky and Kimmy let out relieved sighs.

They had no way of knowing that the rainy day would come so soon.

> Tigers claw!
> Tigers ROAR!
> Send the ball down the floor—
> Two points MORE!

Ivy Blake finished her cheer with a forward flip, landing on her feet. Then she ran off the floor clapping loudly, her long, streaked hair streaming behind her.

Corky and Kimmy watched from the bottom row of the bleachers, making notes on their clipboards. "She's good," Corky said, watching Ivy trot over to the other cheerleading candidates.

"I like her," Kimmy agreed. "She's very strong. Very physical."

Ivy was a big girl, Corky observed. Tall and athletic looking. She had a dramatic face, framed by long wavy hair, brown with blond streaks through it. She wore bright pink lipstick.

"So we've narrowed it down to three girls," Kimmy said, studying her clipboard. Ms. Closter had been called to a teachers' meeting on the third floor. As co-captains, the choice of Hannah's replacement was up to Corky and Kimmy.

Corky nodded. She started to say something else about Ivy. But a man interrupted.

"Hey, girls—get away from the bleachers! Can't you see we're working up here?"

Corky turned and saw two men in blue coveralls at the top of the bleachers, working on the metal frame that supported the wooden benches.

"Sorry!" Corky called up to them. She and Kimmy whispered about the candidates as they stepped away from the bleachers and made their way across the gym floor to the group of girls.

"You were all great!" Corky told them. She could see the tension on their faces. Ivy seemed to be the only one who remained calm. She applied a fresh coat of pink lipstick to her lips as Corky talked.

"We've narrowed it down to three," Corky told them. She glanced down at her clipboard. "Ivy Blake, Lauren Wilson, and Rochelle Drexler."

"We want to thank you all for trying out," Kimmy told them. "You were all terrific. It was a tough choice."

She turned to Ivy, Lauren, and Rochelle. "If you three will stay," Kimmy said. "The rest of you can pick up your stuff and leave. Thanks again for trying out."

A few girls grumbled, disappointed. A couple lingered to congratulate the three finalists. The others hurried over to the far wall to pick up their coats and backpacks.

Corky watched them make their way out of the gym, then turned back to Ivy, Lauren, and Rochelle. "I wish we could take all three of you," she told them. "But we need only one replacement."

"Could you wait over there?" Kimmy asked them, pointing to the bleachers. "Give Corky and me a couple more minutes. I think we're pretty close to a decision. But we may need you to do another cheer or something if there's a tie."

"Don't stand too near the bleachers," Corky warned. "Those men are working up at the top."

Lauren and Rochelle walked across the floor, talking excitedly. Ivy followed behind them, tugging back her long, streaked hair.

Corky and Kimmy made their way into Ms. Closter's small office in the corner of the gym. Kimmy clicked on the light. Corky sat down on the edge of Ms. Closter's cluttered desk. Kimmy leaned against the doorframe.

Through the large window, Corky gazed out at the three girls waiting awkwardly near the bleachers for a decision.

"They all have strengths and weaknesses," Kimmy said. "All three have tried out before and almost made the squad. Lauren used to live next door to me until her family moved to North Hills. Now she and Ivy are best friends."

Corky stared out at Lauren Wilson. She was tall and graceful, with creamy, pale white skin. Her straight auburn hair was pulled back into a short ponytail. She wore a long gray sweatshirt over bright blue leggings.

"Lauren is a great jumper," Corky commented. "But her voice is kind of weak."

Kimmy nodded. "Yeah. Rochelle has the best voice. You can hear her two blocks away!"

Rochelle Drexler wore loose-fitting maroon sweats and a maroon and white Shadyside Tigers cap over her long, white-blond hair. She had a pretty face, perky, with a tiny, upturned nose and round blue eyes.

"Rochelle did a great routine," Kimmy continued, checking her clipboard. "She had the best height on her spread eagles, and her splits were very graceful."

"I'd say it's between Rochelle and Ivy," Corky said thoughtfully, watching the girls through the window. Lauren was trying on Rochelle's cap, twisting it backward, then sideways. Rochelle was sitting cross-legged on the floor, leaning over. Her hair hung down over her face to the floor. She was running a hairbrush down through it, brushing vigorously.

But where was Ivy? Had she wandered off?

"Ivy is really good," Kimmy replied. "Better than Lauren. But she's not as graceful as Rochelle. And Rochelle has a better voice. More spirit too."

"Then we're decided on Rochelle?" Corky asked.

"Yeah, I guess—" Kimmy started to say.

Corky interrupted her with a startled shout. "Hey!" She jumped off the desk and moved to the door.

Kimmy stepped aside—to reveal Ivy standing behind her, just outside the office.

"Ivy—how long have you been standing there?" Corky demanded sharply. "Were you eavesdropping?"

Ivy's pink lips parted in an *O* of surprise. She blushed until her cheeks were nearly as bright as her lips. "No. No way!" she protested.

"Did you hear what we were saying?" Kimmy asked shrilly.

Ivy shook her head. "No. Really, Kimmy, I didn't

hear a word. Honest." She raised her right hand as if swearing an oath.

"Then why were you hiding outside the door?" Corky asked.

"I wasn't hiding!" Ivy declared hotly, still blushing. "I just came to ask if you were going to reach a decision soon. I have a tennis lesson, and my mom is waiting in the car."

"We're almost ready," Kimmy told her. "Go on back with the other two. We'll be right over."

Ivy spun around and began walking slowly toward the bleachers. Kimmy turned back to Corky. "Do you think she overheard what we were saying?"

"It doesn't really matter," Corky replied with a shrug. "We've made our decision, right? The order is: Rochelle, Ivy, Lauren—one, two, three."

"Right," Kimmy agreed. "Let's go tell them."

They stepped out of the office and started toward the bleachers.

Corky stopped and grabbed Kimmy's arm as she heard the man's shout. "Hey—*look out!*"

A girl screamed.

Another man's voice wailed, "Nooooo!"

Corky and Kimmy started running across the floor.

Lauren shrieked in horror. The maroon and white cap fell from her hand.

Corky saw Ivy raise her hands to her cheeks, her pink mouth dropping open in shock.

"What's happening? What?" Corky managed to cry out.

Then her eyes fell on Rochelle. Still cross-legged on the floor. Still leaning over, her hair over her face.

"Ohhhhh!" Corky let out a horrified wail when she saw the bright red gush of blood spurting up from Rochelle's neck.

She saw the blood. And then she saw the screwdriver. Stuck deep into the back of Rochelle's neck.

"Ohhhhh no!" Corky knew at once what had happened. The screwdriver had fallen from the bleachers above.

It had dropped straight down.

And now it lay embedded in the back of Rochelle's neck.

The blood poured out over Rochelle.

The hairbrush fell from her hand.

She slumped forward until her head hit the floor.

She didn't move.

Chapter 8

A SHOCK FROM LAUREN

Corky froze a few steps behind Kimmy, unable to
believe her eyes.

"Call a doctor! Call a doctor! Call a doctor!" Lauren
shrieked, dropping to her knees beside Rochelle.

"But she's dead!" Ivy moaned. Loud sobs escaped
Ivy's throat.

"No, she's not! Quick, call a doctor!" Lauren cried,
bent over Rochelle's unmoving body.

"What's *happened?*" Ms. Closter came rushing into
the gym. She tossed her notebook aside as she saw
Rochelle sprawled facedown on the floor. "So much
blood! Did she fall?"

The cheerleader coach let out a low cry as she

moved close enough to see the screwdriver lodged in Rochelle's neck.

The two workers appeared beside Ms. Closter. "It flew out of my hand!" one of them cried in a trembling voice. "I don't know what happened. I was holding it tight. But it just *flew* out!"

"Corky! Kimmy! Go!" Ms. Closter screamed, pointing frantically to her office. "Call for an ambulance! Hurry! Go!"

"She's losing a lot of blood," one of the workmen muttered.

Corky turned away from Rochelle and, breathing hard, forced herself to run toward the office.

As she turned, she had caught a glimpse of the strange expression on Ivy's face. It lingered in Corky's mind as she ran.

Not a smile, she thought.

No. Not a smile. Ivy wasn't smiling—*was* she?

The paramedics arrived quickly. They stopped the bleeding and hurried Rochelle away on a stretcher. She had lost a lot of blood, but she was breathing.

Corky watched as two police officers questioned the workers. The two men had their heads lowered. One of them was gesturing with his hands, demonstrating how the screwdriver had tumbled.

Two more officers had climbed to the top of the bleachers and were examining the metal frame. A young officer stood at the door, talking to Mr. Hernandez, the principal.

Corky wiped tears off her cheeks with the sleeve of her sweatshirt. She and Kimmy had answered the officers' questions. Now they stood huddled silently beside Ivy and Lauren in front of Ms. Closter's office.

"I—I just can't *believe* it!" Kimmy wailed. "A few minutes ago Rochelle was cheering and shouting and jumping. And then . . ." A choked sob ended her sentence.

"She'll be okay. I'm sure she will," Corky murmured.

Corky lowered her eyes to the floor. She didn't want to start crying again. After she had called for the ambulance, Corky burst into tears. It was a while before she could stop crying.

She knew she wasn't crying for Rochelle. She barely knew Rochelle. Corky was crying for her sister Bobbi.

She couldn't help thinking about her sister now. Bobbi had been a cheerleader too. But Bobbi hadn't been lucky like Rochelle. Bobbi had died in this same gym. In the locker room. In the shower.

Bobbi had been trapped in the shower room. Somehow, the doors had shut and she'd been locked inside. Then scalding hot water shot out of the showers. Unable to escape, Bobbi had suffocated in the boiling steam.

Murdered. Murdered by the evil.

And now another cheerleader had been wounded in a weird accident. More horror.

Was it an accident?

Corky glanced over at Ms. Closter. The police officers continued to question her. "I—I have to call

Rochelle's parents now," Ms. Closter was telling them. "I have to tell them where they're taking Rochelle."

Kimmy had wrapped her arms tightly around herself. Corky saw that she was trying to stop herself from trembling. Ivy and Lauren whispered together, leaning against the wall, their eyes red, their faces pale.

"You girls can go home!" Ms. Closter called. She waved a hand at the door. "I'll call you later to check on you."

Corky took a deep breath, hoisted her backpack, and made her way out into the hall. She and Kimmy stopped outside the door. They exchanged sorrowful glances, but neither of them spoke.

Ivy and Lauren followed, their expressions dazed and glum. Lauren struggled with the sleeve of her jacket. Ivy helped her into it.

Then Ivy turned to Kimmy and Corky. "Uh—this sounds really stupid after—after what happened," she murmured reluctantly. She avoided Corky's eyes. "But do you think you could tell us . . ." She hesitated.

Corky didn't understand what Ivy was trying to ask. "Tell you what?" she demanded. Her voice came out tight and shrill.

"Well . . ." Ivy glanced at Lauren. "Could you tell us which of us won? Who's going to be the new cheerleader?"

Kimmy's mouth dropped open. She let out a gasp.

Ivy blushed. "I—I mean, what happened to Rochelle—it's j-just *horrible!*" she stammered. "I guess I'm still dazed. I still don't believe it happened. But I think it would make me feel better to know—I mean, to know who won."

Lauren nodded in silent agreement.

Corky gaped at them, trying to understand. How could they *care* about cheerleading after a girl had nearly been killed? How could they be so *cold?* Corky asked herself.

Or were they just struggling desperately to return their lives to normal? Trying to think normal thoughts, to force the horror from their minds?

Corky glanced at Kimmy. Kimmy nodded.

"Well, I guess Ivy is the new squad member," Corky told them. Her words came out in a whisper.

"What? What did you say?" Lauren demanded.

"It's Ivy," Corky repeated, forcing her voice a little louder. "The new cheerleader is Ivy."

A smile crossed Ivy's pink lips.

Lauren's chin quivered and her nostrils flared angrily. "This isn't fair, Corky!" she cried. "Really. This isn't fair!"

"Come on, Lauren—" Corky started to say.

"Don't tell me to come on!" Lauren fumed, scowling at Corky. "I know why you didn't choose me. I know why. It's because of Alex and me!"

Chapter 9

BOOM

"**F**irst Hannah, then Rochelle," Debra murmured, frowning. She tucked her toothpick-thin legs under her on the couch.

"Don't start," Corky pleaded. She was slumped sideways on the armchair across from Debra. She raised one foot to stare at a hole in the toe of her white sock.

"Did you feel an evil presence?" Debra demanded, ignoring Corky's demand.

"It was an accident," Corky insisted. "An unbelievable, tragic accident. I—I just feel so bad for Rochelle. She'll probably miss weeks of school."

They sat in Corky's living room. Golden afternoon

sunlight streamed into the front window. Outside, the snow had begun to melt.

"You don't think the evil is back?" Debra persisted. Her sky blue eyes locked on Corky's.

Corky shook her head. "It's too frightening to think about. Please—let's try not to talk about yesterday. Talk about something else."

"I wonder how long they'll keep the gym closed," Debra said, toying with the fringe on one of the pillows. "How are we supposed to practice for the tournament?"

"It's probably just closed for today," Corky replied. She took a long drink from the can of diet Coke she held in one hand. "The police have to do whatever they do."

"They have counselors at school," Debra added. "For kids who want to talk about the accident. You know. Talk about how they feel." She dropped the pillow onto her lap. "Think you should go? You seem really stressed out."

Corky sighed. "I don't need to talk to a counselor," she replied, squeezing the soda can. "I need to talk to Alex. I can't believe Lauren said that to me! I can't believe that Alex—"

"Lauren was just trying to say the meanest thing she could think of," Debra suggested. She ran a hand back through her short blond hair. "She was upset that Ivy won. So she said the first thing that came into her head."

"Think so?" Corky lowered the soda to her lap, her expression thoughtful. "I don't know, Debra. Lauren

56

and Ivy have been friends for a long time. I don't think Lauren would be angry with Ivy—"

"She's angry with *you*—not Ivy," Debra replied.

The phone rang. Corky jumped to her feet, nearly spilling the soda. "Maybe that's Alex. I've called his house twelve times. I left twelve messages for him to call!"

She hurried to the kitchen phone and grabbed the receiver. "Hello?" she asked breathlessly.

"Hi. It's me!"

"Alex—where've you been?" Corky cried, not meaning to sound so frantic.

"Uh—I had some stuff to do. How are you doing, Corky? Are you okay? I heard what happened after school yesterday. To Rochelle."

"I—I guess I'm okay," Corky replied uncertainly. She took a deep breath. "Listen, Alex, there's something I've got to ask you. I'm just going to be blunt and come right to the point, okay?"

He hesitated. "Yeah. Sure. What's the problem?"

"What's with you and Lauren?" Corky blurted out.

"Huh? Lauren?" She couldn't tell if Alex was genuinely confused by the question, or if he was stalling for time.

"Yeah. You and Lauren," she insisted. "Lauren told me that you and she—"

"Whoa!" Alex interrupted. "If she said that we went out or anything, it's a lie."

"You didn't go out with Lauren?" Corky demanded. "What did you do—stay *in* with her?"

Alex let out an uncomfortable laugh. "No. No way,

57

Corky. I helped her one night last week with her government project. That's all. Maybe she got the wrong idea."

"Maybe—" Corky replied. "Listen, Alex, do you want to come over tonight? We could study together. Maybe you could help me with *my* government project."

"Sorry," he answered reluctantly. "I can't. I—uh—just can't tonight, Corky."

Couldn't he think of an excuse? Corky wondered. Even a *lame* excuse would be better than no excuse at all.

They talked for only a few more seconds, then said good bye. After hanging up, Corky lingered in the kitchen. He isn't telling the truth, she thought sadly. There's definitely something going on.

When she returned to the living room, she was startled to find Naomi there. Still in her red and blue ski jacket, Naomi had dropped down into Corky's chair and was talking heatedly to Debra.

"If we can't practice, we can't do the fire baton routine," Naomi was saying. "It's going to take a lot of work—especially with a new girl on the squad."

Both girls raised their eyes to Corky as she entered the living room. "Naomi, I didn't hear you come in," Corky said.

"How are you? Okay?" Naomi asked. "Kimmy said that you and Debra were here, so I—"

"Want a diet Coke or something?" Corky offered. "Take off your jacket."

Naomi unzipped the jacket but didn't pull it off. The pale late-afternoon sun through the window made her fiery-red hair glow. "Did you hear about Lauren?" she asked.

Corky lowered herself onto the arm of the couch. "Huh? What about her?"

"She went to Ms. Closter and begged to be an alternate," Naomi replied.

"An alternate? We've never had an alternate before."

Naomi nodded. "I know. But she got Ms. Closter to agree to it. Lauren will be like the seventh member of the squad. She told Ms. Closter she'd come to every practice and learn all the routines. Just in case—"

"Just in case *what?*" Corky demanded.

"In case something bad happens to one of us," Naomi replied softly. "Then Lauren would be ready to take her place."

"What else could happen?" Debra declared, rolling her eyes.

"Lauren said it was Ivy's idea," Naomi revealed.

Corky shook her head. "Well, fine," she said. "If being an alternate will make Lauren happy—fine. But Debra is right. The worst has already happened. Nothing else is going to happen to us. Right?"

"Right," Debra and Naomi replied in unison.

A tisket, a tasket,
We want a BASKET!
A tisket, a tasket—

"Ow!" Heather cried. "Stop!"

The other cheerleaders landed heavily, still cheering.

Heather hobbled away from the line, holding her left calf. "Ow! *Man!*" she moaned.

"Heather—what's wrong?" Ms. Closter hurried up to her.

"Just a leg cramp," Heather groaned, bending to rub the calf. "There. It's better." She shook her head. "What a sharp pain!"

"Should I step in for her?" Lauren called from the sidelines.

"It won't be necessary," Ms. Closter replied. "I think you know this routine well enough. I want to drag out the confetti cannons and see if we can get them to work."

Corky glanced up at the gym clock. Eight-twenty. Thursday night. The cheerleaders seldom had night practices. But Ms. Closter had called this one since they'd had a couple of days off. And since the pep rally for the tournament was scheduled for the following day, the last day of school before winter vacation.

Corky smiled as Heather flashed her a thumbs-up sign and returned to the other girls. The practice had started slowly.

I think everyone is uncomfortable being back in the gym, Corky told herself. Every time we glance up at the bleachers, we're reminded of what happened to Rochelle.

But once they'd warmed up with a long aerobics routine followed by some double cartwheels and several cheers, the girls seemed to be in the right spirit.

"Ivy is really a fast learner," Kimmy whispered to Corky. "She already knows some of the routines better than Naomi."

"Yeah, she's good," Corky agreed.

Lauren worked out with the cheerleaders too, staying at the end of the line, concentrating hard on the others, trying to pick up the moves and learn the words. She and Corky avoided each other's eyes. Corky couldn't forget what Lauren had said about Alex.

"Corky? Kimmy? Come help me," Ms. Closter instructed. The three of them rolled the large cannons to the middle of the gym floor and pointed them at the empty bleachers.

"Hope these work," Ms. Closter muttered. "We borrowed them from the college. They use them at pep rallies all the time."

The cheerleaders huddled around as Ms. Closter explained how the cannons worked. "They're loaded," she told them. "Filled with confetti. You just aim them at the bleachers, pull the string, and— *boom!* The confetti flies all over everyone."

"We're not going to fire them off tonight, are we?" Naomi asked.

"Yes, I think we have to," Ms. Closter replied. "To make sure they're working. They're only half loaded. The custodian promised to clean it up tomorrow morning and fill the cannons up all the way."

Ms. Closter probably had to promise the custodian

free tickets to the tournament, Corky thought. He'd never agree to do all that work for nothing.

"Now I want three girls doing handsprings and three girls handling the cannons," Ms. Closter instructed. She pointed to three girls—Kimmy, Debra, and Ivy. "You're handsprings. The others are cannons."

Corky heard disappointed groans. Everyone wanted to fire the cannons.

"Now we'll start with the Hoop cheer," Ms. Closter continued. "Do it twice. Then instead of the usual ending, go into the handsprings. Pull the cords as soon as they finish their handsprings. The confetti will shoot out then."

"This is hard!" Debra complained. "I mean, the timing—"

"Wait! Nobody move!" Naomi shouted, raising both hands. "I dropped a contact! Don't move!"

Everyone groaned. The lenses were constantly popping out of Naomi's eyes!

"There it is. Right beside your sneaker," Lauren told Naomi, pointing to the floor.

"Hey—thanks!" Naomi bent and retrieved the contact lens. "You've got good eyes!" She struggled to replace the lens. "I've really got to get new ones. These just don't fit."

"Let's try to get the timing down," Ms. Closter told them, tossing her whistle behind her. "It's not as hard as it sounds. It's just a matter of pulling the strings as soon as the cheer ends."

Corky turned when she heard angry voices behind her. Ivy and Heather, she saw, seemed to be having an argument. "How can I?" Heather was saying. "My leg is still sore from that cramp."

Kimmy moved quickly, stepping between them. "What's the problem, Heather?"

"I really think I should handle the cannon," Ivy broke in before Heather could reply. "My handsprings aren't that sharp. I'm going to look like a total klutz."

Heather shook her head. "No way, Ivy. I really want to do the cannon. I'm sorry, but—"

Ivy tossed up her hands and let out an exasperated groan. "Okay, okay. If you're going to make a big deal about it!" she fumed. She stomped away from Heather.

Temper, temper, Corky thought, surprised by Ivy's outburst.

She's the new girl, Corky thought, watching Ivy's angry expression. She's not going to impress anyone by going nuts over something like this.

"Are we ready now?" Ms. Closter asked quietly, raising her eyes to the scoreboard clock. The adviser always stayed out of these arguments, letting the cheerleaders settle them themselves. "It's getting late. I know you all have homework to do when you get home."

"Line up, everyone!" Kimmy called out.

"We do the Hoop cheer as we always do?" Debra asked.

Ms. Closter nodded. "No change. Just at the end.

The three girls do their handsprings from right to left in front of the cannons. As they finish, the cannons go off and shoot their confetti."

There were more questions. Mostly about timing. Then Ms. Closter helped position Corky, Heather, and Naomi. "Hold the cords firmly so you'll be ready."

Corky glanced down the row of cheerleaders. Everyone seemed to be ready. She was glad to see that Ivy's smile had returned. In fact, she was beaming.

Kimmy gave the signal, and they went into the cheer:

> HOOP—there it is!
> HOOP—there it is
> TWO points!

Then into the handsprings with Kimmy in the lead.

Corky gave her cord a sharp pull, triggering her cannon.

She looked over to see if the others were successful.

She had turned just in time to see Heather's cannon backfire.

The cannon exploded with a roar that shook the gym.

Heather had no time to react.

The blast snapped her head back.

Her hands shot out helplessly, and she appeared to fly backward.

And then she toppled onto her back on the floor and didn't move.

Chapter 10

POISON IVY?

Corky reached Heather first. She dropped down beside her on the floor and grabbed her hand. "Heather—are you okay? Can you hear me? Heather?" Corky cried.

The other cheerleaders formed a tight circle around them. Ms. Closter burst through the circle, her face tight with concern. "Stand back! Give her some air!"

Heather slowly opened her eyes. She stared up at Corky, blinking, her expression dazed. "What?" she uttered, gazing up blankly at Corky as if she didn't recognize her.

Ms. Closter edged Corky out of the way. She leaned over Heather and started asking her questions:

"What's your name? What's my name? How old are you? What's the name of this school?"

Heather answered the questions promptly. Then she groaned and pulled herself up to a sitting position. She touched her red cheek. "Ouch!"

"Powder burns," Ms. Closter told her softly. "Your cannon backfired."

The cheerleader coach helped Heather to her feet. Heather straightened her hair, then rubbed the back of her neck. "I—I'm okay," she announced uncertainly. "I think I was mostly scared."

I think we're *all* scared now, Corky thought darkly.

The practice session ended a few minutes later. Corky hurried to the student parking lot to her car. She wanted to get away—away from everyone, somewhere where she could think.

She pulled her car door open and started to slide in. But Kimmy and Debra came running after her. "Hey, Corky—wait! We have to talk!" Kimmy called.

It was a clear, cold night. A pale moon hung low over the bare trees. The air was still. At the end of the lot Corky saw a black cat squeeze through the wire fence.

"I already know what you're going to say," Corky told her two friends. She sat sideways in the driver's seat with her feet on the ground. Kimmy and Debra huddled in the open car doorway.

"We have to talk about it," Kimmy repeated breathlessly. She rewrapped her wool muffler around her neck. Her forehead was still covered with perspiration from the hot gym.

"You've got to face the facts, Corky," Debra insisted heatedly.

"I don't want to face anything," Corky shot back. "I just want to go home and take a shower."

"Corky—did you notice the smile on Ivy's face?" Kimmy demanded. "Did you see the smile on her face just before the cannon strings were pulled?"

"Really, Kimmy—" Corky started to say.

But Debra interrupted. "Let's begin at the beginning," she said, her eyes burning into Corky's. "Let's just make a list, okay?"

Corky sighed. "I can see you're not going to give me a break."

"Corky, you agreed with me when I said that the evil was back!" Kimmy accused. "Now you don't even want to talk about it. Why?"

"Let's just make a list," Debra repeated calmly. "One: Hannah is in a horrible car accident. That makes room for Ivy on the cheerleader squad. Two: Ivy doesn't get picked. Ivy overhears you and Kimmy choosing Rochelle. Suddenly Rochelle has a horrible accident and is sent to the hospital. Two horrible accidents—and now Ivy is on the squad."

"Debra—this is crazy!" Corky cried. She turned to Kimmy. "You don't believe what Debra is saying, do you? You don't believe that Ivy is possessed by the evil? Even if Ivy *is* causing these accidents it doesn't mean that the evil is back."

Kimmy shrugged. "I don't know what to think, Corky. Let Debra finish."

Corky shivered. She wanted to close the car door and roar away. "We're all going to catch our death out here," she muttered.

"Catch our death. For sure," Debra repeated bitterly. "Item number three: Ivy's best friend is Lauren, right? And Lauren desperately wants to join the squad. So what happens tonight? Accident number three. Heather is practically blown to bits. Lauren *almost* made the team."

"You're saying that Ivy made the cannon backfire?" Corky asked, shivering again. Was it the cold, or was it Debra's words that were giving her chills?

Debra nodded. "We all saw Ivy argue with Heather about working the cannon. She must have known Heather would refuse, which would give her an excuse later. Then we all saw the smile on her face just before the strings were pulled. What was she smiling about, Corky? What?"

Corky didn't reply. She felt a wave of sadness wash over her. Fighting the evil was too hard, too dangerous, too terrifying. She had already drowned it once. She didn't want to face it again.

"You haven't proven anything, Debra," she said, reaching for the door handle and turning to face the wheel. "We have to believe that they've all been accidents. We *have* to believe that. Otherwise— otherwise—*it's just too frightening!*" she cried out, startled by her own emotion.

"Listen to me, Corky," Debra insisted softly.

"No!" Corky cried. "Stop, Debra. Just stop! You *want* to believe the evil is back. You think it's really exciting and fascinating! It's a game to you and Kimmy! You didn't lose a sister to the evil! You didn't lose a sister you loved. I think about her every day of my life!"

Hot tears rolled down Corky's face. Her entire body trembled. "I miss Bobbi so much! I think about her every hour!" Corky said, sobbing. "I think about my poor sister and the horrible way she died. And I don't want the evil to be back! I want it all to be *accidents,* Debra! All accidents!"

Debra's expression softened. "Sorry," she murmured.

Kimmy bent down to hug Corky. "I'm sorry, Corky. It's just that—"

"How long can we ignore it?" Debra asked, keeping her voice soft. "How many accidents will it take, Corky? Ivy is going to get Lauren on the squad. I *know* it. The next accident, it—it could happen to one of us."

Debra took a breath, then added, "It could happen to *you.*"

Startled, Corky gazed up at her friend.

Why did Debra say it that way? Corky wondered.

Why did it sound so much like a threat?

Chapter 11

A HOT ROUTINE

*A*s she pulled up to her house, Corky spotted a familiar car in the driveway. "I don't believe it," she said, surprised. "What is Alex doing here?"

She found him wrestling on the living room floor with her brother, Sean. Alex was sprawled facedown on the carpet, pounding the floor with one fist. Sean straddled his back, twisting Alex's other arm up behind him as far as it would go.

"Okay! Okay! I give!" Alex cried, red faced, his blond hair standing up in all directions.

"Two out of three falls!" Sean declared gleefully, triumphantly rolling off Alex's back.

They both turned as Corky stepped into the center

of the room. "Aw, why'd *you* have to come home?" Sean cried angrily.

"I'm glad to see you too!" Corky shot back. She tossed her coat onto a chair.

Alex climbed to his feet, pulling his gray sweatshirt down over his faded jeans. He grinned at Corky. "Sean and I were just working out a little."

"I beat his butt!" Sean declared. He turned at the doorway and flexed both biceps. Corky had to laugh. Her brother had such skinny arms!

"Guess you two want me to leave," Sean said, grinning. "So you can go smoochy-smoochy."

Corky laughed. "Where'd you hear *that?*"

"On TV," Sean replied, and disappeared upstairs to his room.

Alex dropped onto the couch. He tried to smooth his hair into place, using both hands. "How was practice?"

"You wouldn't believe it," Corky replied, rolling her eyes. Sitting down on the other end of the couch, she told him about Heather's accident.

"Weird," Alex murmured, shaking his head. "Are you okay, Corky?"

She nodded. "I'm surprised to see you here, Alex. Shouldn't you be helping Lauren with her government project? Or helping Deena Martinson with her French or something?"

Alex shrugged. "Can I help it if I'm a genius?"

She saw his cheeks turn pink. One hand tapped the couch arm nervously. "Well, I'm real glad to see you,"

71

Corky admitted, her expression softening. "How come you came over?"

He shrugged again. "Just wondered how you were doing." His eyes darted around the room, then returned to her. "It's hard to settle down and do my homework. I'm stoked! I mean, I can't stop thinking about the tournament."

Corky sighed. "I've been looking forward to it too," she told him, clasping her hands tightly in her lap. "But these horrible accidents . . ." Her voice trailed off.

"I know," he replied softly. His hand continued to tap the couch arm. He kept shifting his weight, crossing and uncrossing his legs.

Why is he so nervous? Corky wondered.

"Maybe the pep rally after school tomorrow will help you get into it," he suggested.

"Maybe," she replied without enthusiasm. "We have some great new cheers. And we're going to turn off all the lights in the gym and do Naomi's fire baton routine."

"Cool," Alex said. He cleared his throat. The pink circles on his cheeks grew darker. She saw him hesitate. He seemed to be working up his courage. "Corky, I want to tell you something," he started to say.

Corky felt her heart skip a beat. *He came over here to break up with me!* she realized.

I can't believe he's doing this! Right before the tournament. Right before Christmas.

She felt her face go hot. Her mouth suddenly felt

dry as cotton. She didn't want to break up. She really cared about him.

"What is it, Alex?" she managed to choke out.

"Well, I've been meaning to tell you," he said, tapping the couch arm. I—uh—"

The doorbell rang.

Corky leapt up from the couch. "Who could *that* be?" she fretted, hurrying to the front door.

She glanced back at Alex. Did he look disappointed that he didn't get to say what was on his mind? Or relieved? She couldn't tell.

Corky pulled open the front door, and Jay came bursting in. He wore a heavy red plaid ski sweater with the collar and one sleeve ripped. His baggy, faded jeans had holes in both knees. His Mighty Ducks cap was pulled sideways on his head.

"Jay!" Corky cried in surprise.

He grinned and pushed past her into the living room. Then, without another word, he spread his legs, raised his arms, and went into an enthusiastic cheer.

> Give me a C!
> Give me an O!
> Give me an R!
> Give me a K!
> Give me a Y!
> What's that spell?
> I don't KNOW!

Alex shut his eyes and shook his head. Corky laughed.

"Did I spell it right?" Jay asked Corky. "I'm not as good a speller as Alex, the brain."

"What are you doing here?" Alex demanded.

Jay flashed his toothy grin. "Hey—you know what they say? Two's company, three's a *party!*"

Corky laughed and took her place on the couch. At least Alex won't break up with me while Jay is here, she told herself.

She glanced at Alex.

But what will happen when Alex and I are alone? she wondered sadly.

"It's going really well!" Kimmy shouted excitedly over the roar from the bleachers. "Everyone is really *pumped!*"

Corky flashed her a thumbs-up sign and hurried to take her place in line for the Hoop cheer. She stared up at the bleachers, filled with cheering, shouting, clapping Shadyside kids.

This is the loudest pep rally ever! Corky thought happily. Even Mr. Hernandez couldn't bring everyone down with his boring speech about how we have to be good citizens at the tournament because we represent Shadyside at all times.

As soon as the principal ended his short speech, the bleachers rang out. The kids all jumped to their feet, eager to start cheering, eager to show their support for the Tigers. And when the team members were introduced and came trotting across the gym floor, the kids erupted in an explosion of sound that shook the room.

We don't have to urge the crowd to yell today,

Corky thought. There'll be a lot of sore throats and hoarse voices when *this* pep rally ends!

The new rap cheer had driven them wild. The bleachers sagged and rocked as everyone joined in. The routine was such a hit, the cheerleaders were forced to perform it three times!

Corky soared up into her spread eagle now. A very high jump after "A Tisket, a Tasket."

Amazing, what a little adrenaline can do! Corky told herself.

Legs straight out. Perfect! Down now, into a split. Yes!

She glanced down the line of girls. Everyone was looking good!

Up now—and repeat the cheer.

The shouts roared over her. The gym appeared to shimmer and shake under the bright lights. Can these old walls take it? Corky wondered.

She pictured the walls crumbling, the bleachers crashing as everyone continued to shout and clap.

But the frightening image vanished as she and Kimmy did side-by-side cartwheels.

They finished the routine with a forward flip. The cheers rang out even louder. Corky could see Ms. Closter against the gym wall, a pleased smile on her face.

And now the big finish! Corky thought.

The fire batons.

"Let's light the flame of victory!" Kimmy was shouting into the floor microphone. "This will be our last cheer of the afternoon. So let's hear you! Let's keep the energy up for the whole tournament! Let the Tigers know you're behind them!"

Corky lined up behind Naomi to receive her lighted baton. Ivy had been assigned the job of lighting them.

"This is *amazing!*" Naomi cried.

"It's unbelievable!" Heather shouted, right behind Corky. "I've never seen the school so totally pumped!"

"Go, Tigers!" Corky shouted. Eager to begin the new routine, she turned to Ivy.

Against the wall, Ivy grabbed a fire baton from the pile. She dipped one end in the bucket of kerosene in front of her, turned the baton, and dipped the other end. Then, holding the baton in the middle, she lighted both ends with a plastic lighter.

First in line, Debra took the flaming baton from Ivy, handling it carefully, holding it straight out in front of her. She twirled it slowly. The twin balls of fire circled each other in the air.

Naomi took the next baton. Corky waited patiently for Ivy to light the next.

The crowd quieted in anticipation. The lights went out as Ivy lighted the last baton and, twirling it slowly, took her place in line.

The gym grew quiet as the cheerleaders raised the batons over their heads and twirled them. Corky glanced down the row as she twirled. The batons made rings of fire, bright, flaming rings that danced and spun in the silent darkness.

When Corky heard the sharp, high-pitched cries, she thought at first it was the squeal of a puppy.

"Ai! Ai! Ai! Ai!"

But turning toward the sound, she saw the bright yellow flames trickle down Naomi's sleeve. As the flames leapt over Naomi's sweater and skirt, Corky realized that the sharp, terrified squeals were coming from Naomi.

The tiny cries were quickly drowned out by the horrified shouts and moans from the bleachers.

Chapter 12

IVY ON THIN ICE

"Kimmy, you were so brave," Corky declared. "I just stood there. But you—you risked your life."

Kimmy frowned. "If you want to know the truth, I didn't think about it at all. I saw Naomi on fire, and I just jumped on her, knocked her to the floor, and tried to smother the flames."

Debra shook her head. "Don't be modest. You saved Naomi's life. She's badly burned. But you stopped the flames before they reached her face."

Kimmy sighed. "I don't even remember it. It all happened so fast."

Corky and her two friends walked on in silence. Dressed in coats and mufflers and wool caps, they trudged through the park, under bare trees, over patches of lingering snow.

The red ball of a sun didn't beam down any warmth. Corky shivered and stuffed her hands deeper into her coat pockets. Her breath steamed up in white puffs in front of her.

"Look—a rabbit!" Debra pointed between the trees.

Corky saw a small brown creature dart into a pile of dead leaves. "Didn't anyone tell him it's winter?" she muttered.

Shadyside Park stretched behind the high school, its woods sloping all the way down to the river. Corky spotted the remains of a kite caught high in a tree branch. Ice clung to the frame, making it sparkle like an enormous diamond.

Kimmy and Debra had appeared at her house right after breakfast on Saturday morning. They had insisted on a serious talk. Corky wasn't surprised to see them. But she felt cooped up and uncomfortable in the house.

So here they were, crunching through the woods, the only people for miles, talking about everything except the real subject on their minds—Ivy. And the accidents.

"Naomi will be in the hospital for weeks," Kimmy reported, stepping over a fallen tree trunk. "That means that Lauren is on the squad."

"Ivy gets her wish," Debra murmured.

"You mean *Lauren* gets her wish," Corky corrected

her. She pulled off the wool cap and shook out her blond hair. The cap always made her head itch.

"You think Lauren is inhabited by the evil?" Debra asked. "You think Lauren is the one who's been knocking off the cheerleaders one by one?"

"I don't," Kimmy replied after a few seconds. She brushed against a prickly shrub. Several burrs stuck to the sleeve of her coat. "Ivy is the one who dipped the fire batons. She's the one who made sure that kerosene ran all over Naomi's baton."

"She swore it wasn't her fault," Corky reported, helping Kimmy pull the burrs off her coat sleeve. "Did you see Ivy crying her eyes out when Ms. Closter questioned her? She swore she was careful."

"If Lauren is possessed by the evil, she could be trying to make Ivy look guilty," Debra said.

Corky tossed the last burr to the ground. She turned to her two friends. "Does it really matter which one of them it is?" she cried. "We *know* the evil is back. We all agree on that—right? After what happened to Naomi, we all agree that it's back!"

Kimmy and Debra nodded solemnly.

"So what does that mean?" Corky continued heatedly. "It means that—"

She stopped when she heard the voice. A girl's voice. Nearby.

They all heard it.

Peering through the maze of tree trunks, Corky saw that they had walked near the bank of the river. The shiny white ground she spied just beyond the trees was actually solid ice.

She heard a girl's high-pitched laugh.

Then she saw a flash of blue against the white.

Who was out there? Who was on the ice?

Motioning to the others to be silent, Corky led the way toward the shore. Using the tree trunks as cover, they crept close enough to see the shore clearly, and the river stretching out beyond it, silvery and sparkling in the sunlight.

Another flash of blue.

Corky saw a girl in a down vest over a blue sweater, skating in a small area on the ice.

Another girl, in a bright red sweater and matching muffler, stood a few feet from the shore, hands in her jeans pockets, watching the other girl skate.

Corky recognized Lauren first. She was the one watching.

Then she recognized Ivy's long, streaked hair swirling behind her as she skated. Ivy's blades made sharp slicing sounds as she twisted and turned, skating strange patterns, her arms swinging out in front of her.

"It's Ivy!" Kimmy whispered. "What is she *doing?* Why is she skating like that?"

Corky didn't reply. Peering out from behind a tree trunk, she watched Ivy skate—sharp turns and quick reverses, then repeating the patterns again and again.

Lauren watched intently from the shore, standing motionless on the ice, motionless and silent.

"I don't believe this! This is so *weird!*" Kimmy whispered.

"I think she's skating some kind of symbol," Debra suggested, hiding behind Corky, her hands on Corky's shoulders. "See how she keeps repeating the same thing?"

Corky gasped when she saw the white steam funneling up behind Ivy. Squinting hard at the sparkling ice, she saw the small hole in the surface. The steam poured straight up from the hole.

And now Ivy was skating around the steam hole, around and around it, skating faster and faster until she became a blue blur in the billowing smoke.

"This proves it!" Corky whispered to her two friends. She felt a chill run down her body, making her entire body tremble. "This proves it. Ivy is the evil!"

"What are we going to *do?*" Kimmy cried, unable to hide her fear. "She sent Hannah and Naomi and Rochelle to the hospital. We could be next." Her chin trembled. A sob escaped her throat. "What are we going to *do?*"

"I think I have a plan," Debra said softly. She lowered her voice even more. "We have to drown her."

Chapter 13

A SURPRISE FROM SANTA

Corky reached for the phone, then lowered her hand to her lap. Come on—call him! she urged herself. You've been staring at that phone for twenty minutes!

She spun around as the door to her bedroom swung open. "Are you busy?" Sean demanded. He had some kind of purple fruit roll-up hanging out of his mouth.

"Yes. I'm on the phone," Corky replied sharply.

"No, you're not," he insisted.

"Well, I'm going to be. Beat it," she told him. She picked up the receiver and waited for him to leave.

"You stink!" he called, slamming the door behind him.

Corky felt guilty. She knew she was taking out her anxiety on Sean.

Go ahead and call Alex, she told herself, staring at the phone. What's your problem? You've called him a thousand times.

She knew what the problem was. She didn't want Alex to break up with her. She had avoided him ever since school had let out for winter vacation. She was so afraid that if they started to talk, he'd finish what he'd started to say at her house that Thursday night.

And she would be without a boyfriend.

But now she had no choice. She had to call to ask him to the party.

With a heavy feeling in her stomach, she punched in the familiar number. Alex picked up after the second ring. "Hello?"

"Hi, Alex. It's me."

A short silence. She had surprised him, she figured. "Corky? What's up?"

"I thought maybe you'd be at basketball practice," she said awkwardly.

"I've got to leave in a minute," he replied. "It's supposed to be vacation, right? But Coach Hall has scheduled a practice every night. We're all going to be totally wrecked before the tournament starts."

Corky let out a short laugh. "We've been practicing too. We had to come up with a new routine to replace the fire batons. Ms. Closter decided they were too dangerous."

"I guess," Alex replied.

He seems distant, Corky thought. Maybe he's just in a hurry to get to practice.

Can I really do this? Can I ask him to this party? If he says no, I'll *know* he's breaking up with me.

She cleared her throat. "Uh—Alex—Debra and Kimmy and I—we're having a party," she started to say.

"At your house?" he asked. She heard him turn away from the phone and shout something to his mother. "I'm *going,* Mom!"

"It's a Christmas party," Corky continued. Her hand suddenly throbbed. She realized she was squeezing the receiver too tightly. "We thought it'd be nice to have it before we all go up to New Foster for the tournament. An ice-skating party. At the river."

"Huh? At night?" He sounded confused.

"Tomorrow afternoon. It'll be real pretty," Corky told him. "We're going to have Christmas music to skate to, and hot cider, and—"

"Weird idea," he muttered.

"We're inviting all the kids we know, cheerleaders and everyone on the basketball team," she added. "So do you want to come? With me?"

"Yeah. Sure," he replied casually. "Sounds awesome. I've got to get moving, Corky. Talk to you later, okay?"

Corky said good bye and hung up. She realized her hands were cold and clammy. Her heart raced.

Well, you're right, Alex, she thought wistfully, staring out at the darkness beyond her bedroom window. It's going to be an awesome party, for sure.

Everyone should have a really good time.

Everyone except Ivy.

By the time Corky arrived at the river, kids were already skating. "Winter Wonderland" floated out from Kimmy's tape player. Corky saw several kids lined up at the food table, holding cups of steaming hot cider.

"Corky—where *were* you?" Debra came running up to greet her, her plaid wool muffler flying up as she made her way over the fresh snow. Debra wore a blue down vest over a long white sweater and black leggings. "Kimmy and I have been frantic! We thought you changed your mind and chickened out."

"No," Corky replied, her boots sinking into the soft snow as she hurried toward Debra. "It's Alex's fault. He was supposed to pick me up. Then he called at the last minute and said there was something he had to do. I was already late, and then my mom's car wouldn't start."

"Has Alex been acting weird lately, or is it my imagination?" Debra asked, grabbing Corky's hand and tugging her toward the ice.

She's noticed it too, Corky thought unhappily. "Yeah. Alex is definitely weird," Corky muttered. She gazed up at the sky. "Think it's going to snow more?"

Heavy gray clouds blanketed the sky. A gusting wind carried a chill off the frozen river.

"The radio said we're going to get another three inches," Debra reported. She swept her mittened hand out over the river. "Look. Just about everyone is here. Great party, huh?" She waved at Kimmy, who waved back from behind the cider table.

I can't believe Debra is in such a good mood, Corky thought. She's so excited and happy. Has she forgotten why we're giving this party? Has she forgotten what we're about to do?

"Where's Ivy?" Corky asked, her eyes moving from skater to skater out on the ice.

"Over there. With Lauren," Debra replied, her smile fading. "What do you think they're talking about? Which cheerleader they're going to hurt next?"

Corky tugged her skates off her shoulder and followed Debra to the cider table. The song on the tape player changed to "Rudolph the Red-Nosed Reindeer." Some of the guys began singing along at the top of their lungs, deliberately off key.

A gust of wind blew a powdery sheet of snow across the ice. Corky kept her eyes on Ivy and Lauren. On skates, Ivy appeared nearly as tall as the basketball players. Her long hair toppled down from a red and white headband. She wore a snug-fitting bright red ski outfit. Even from a distance Corky could see Ivy's bright pink lips move rapidly as she talked to Lauren.

Lauren wore a fleece-lined denim jacket with the fleece collar pulled up, and faded jeans. She tossed back her head and laughed gleefully as Ivy continued talking.

"Finally!" Kimmy cried as Corky stepped up to the table.

"Sorry," Corky replied. "Alex hung me up." She took a deep sniff. "Mmmmmm. The cider smells great."

"I put a lot of mulling spices in," Kimmy told her, stirring the cider pot with a big ladle. "Excellent party, huh?"

"Yeah. Excellent," Corky replied without any enthusiasm. She leaned close to Kimmy to whisper, "You and Debra seem so cheerful. It's like you forgot what we're doing here."

"We haven't forgotten," Kimmy whispered back, gazing out at Ivy and Lauren. "We're just trying to act normal. We don't want anyone to get suspicious."

Ivy and Lauren were enjoying another good laugh. Three basketball players formed a line and started skating side by side, deliberately trying to knock other kids over. Heather Diehl, wearing an enormous brown and black wool coat, skated gracefully in wide circles. She looked like a pro.

Kimmy held up the ladle. "Want a cup of cider?"

"Maybe later," Corky replied, a chill of fear running down her back.

Are we really going to do this? she wondered. Are we really going to reveal in front of everyone that Ivy is the evil?

"Did Debra bring the book?" she whispered to Kimmy.

Kimmy nodded solemnly. "It's in her car. She's going to get it as soon as everyone arrives."

"Maybe I'll skate a little first," Corky told her. She

sat on the ground to pull off her shoes and lace up her skates.

A little exercise will keep me from getting too scared, she told herself. Maybe if I skate, it'll keep me from thinking about what we're going to do.

A few minutes later she stepped onto the ice and began to skate out onto the frozen river. Her skates slid over the powdery surface, making a pleasant *slush slush* sound.

She had skated for only a few steps, when a figure quickly moved up beside her. "Hey—Corky! When did you get here?"

She braked a little too hard and nearly toppled forward. "Jay! Hi!" she cried, grabbing his arm to steady herself.

He flashed her his toothy grin. He had his Mighty Ducks cap on, as usual. His maroon and white Shadyside High jacket was unsnapped, revealing a gray sweatshirt underneath. "The skating's a little rough because of the snow," he said. "You've got to use a lot of leg power. Watch."

He went into a crazy dance, thrashing his arms over his head as his legs kicked back and forth. "Whooooa!" He let out a long cry as he fell heavily and slid several feet, almost knocking Heather over.

"Nice move, Landers!" Heather called to him, skating around his outstretched body. "Get some training wheels!"

Corky was laughing too hard to help Jay up. "Are you okay?" she finally managed to ask as he skated back beside her.

"Falling down is my hobby," he replied, straightening his cap. "I love it." He brushed snow off his jeans. "Where's Alex?"

Corky slapped at the snow on the back of his jacket. "I don't know. He said he'd be late."

She caught a gleam of excitement in Jay's eyes. "Then you can skate with me," he said eagerly.

Corky laughed. "No way! I don't have your style!"

Jay let out his high-pitched giggle. He took her arm. "Come on. I'll skate normal."

"What's Alex's problem anyway?" Corky asked.

Jay reacted with surprise. "Huh? What do you mean?"

"Why has he been acting so weird lately? I mean, he never seems to be around."

She watched Jay's cheeks redden. "I don't know," he replied. "Really."

He's lying, Corky decided. Jay knows what's going on. But he's being a good friend to Alex. He doesn't want to tell me.

"Hey—Gary!" Jay cupped his hands around his mouth as he shouted across the ice to Gary Brandt. He turned back to Corky. "Listen, I've got to talk to Gary. Let's skate later—okay? I mean, if Alex doesn't show."

He blushed again.

Does Jay know where Alex is? Corky wondered. Is Alex off somewhere with another girl? Is that why Jay is so uncomfortable?

"Yeah. See you later," Corky said. She watched him skate away.

The clouds lowered and the sky darkened. The wind sliced off the ice. The cold crept into Corky's body.

Leaning forward, she skated slowly away from the others. Her legs felt heavy, as if her dread were weighing her down.

The time is getting close, Corky realized. The time to draw out Ivy and all her evil.

The ice stretched ahead of her. A sharp gust of wind pushed at her.

The music faded. Turning back toward shore, Corky saw that she had skated far out. Maybe I'll keep skating and never turn back, she thought.

Just skate away, skate forever.

She suddenly felt dizzy. The ice tilted up in front of her.

"Ohh." She shut her eyes and slowed to a stop.

It's Ivy, she told herself. Thinking about the evil inside Ivy is making me dizzy.

She leaned down, lowered her hands to her knees, waited for the dizziness to pass.

And as she waited, she heard the soft, steady sound of skates cutting into the ice.

Turning toward the sound, Corky saw the dark figure sliding rapidly toward her. She straightened up. Blinked.

Am I seeing things?

No. She was staring at a Santa Claus.

The wind ruffled his bushy white beard. His long red cap waved behind him. His eyes—his eyes glowered menacingly at Corky.

"Hey, Santa!" she cried out as she saw him raise his

hand high over his head. And then she saw the shiny dagger clasped in his hand.

No, not a dagger. A long, pointed icicle. Sharp as a dagger.

No time to move. No time to skate away.

Only time to scream as the Santa uttered a fierce grunt and started to lower the icicle to her throat.

Chapter 14

PARTY TIME

Corky stumbled, raised her hands as she staggered back.

The icicle fell from the Santa's hand and shattered against the ice. The Santa grabbed Corky to stop her fall.

"I'm sorry," he said. "Are you okay?"

"Alex?"

"Corky, I'm really sorry. Didn't you know it was me? I was sure you recognized me!" He pulled off the white beard. She could see his face clearly now, his features expressing his concern.

"You—you really scared me!" she stammered, her chest heaving. She sucked in a deep lungful of air to steady herself.

Alex held on to her with both hands. "I didn't mean to. Really. I was just goofing. I thought you recognized me. I was so stupid, Corky. I'm sorry."

"Why are you wearing this tacky costume?" Corky demanded, starting to feel a little more normal. "Where did you get it?"

"My dad had it up in the attic," Alex told her. "That's why I'm late. He helped me put it on, but it took forever. I thought it would be funny."

"Huh?" She gaped at him.

"You've been so down lately," Alex continued. "So many weird things have happened. You *said* it was a Christmas party. I wanted to give you a laugh."

A smile spread across Corky's face. That was so *sweet* of Alex, she thought.

Impulsively, she grabbed his head, pulled it toward hers, and kissed him. His lips felt warm against hers. She held him for a long time, kissing him, unwilling to move, unwilling to let go, wishing she could stay out on the ice with him forever.

Over his shoulder she could see Kimmy and Debra on the shore. They were both waving to her, calling to her.

Time to begin.

Corky's entire body shook with a sudden tremor of fear.

"Are you cold?" Alex asked, still holding on to her. His red Santa hat slid off his head. He turned to catch it.

"I—I want to go back," she told him. "I have to help Debra and Kimmy."

"Help them?"

"With the party," she replied, starting to skate back toward the others. "We're the hosts, remember?"

"Catch you in a few minutes," he called, strapping the white beard back over his face. "Santa is going to pay a visit on Jay."

"Ho-ho-ho!" Corky called back. She wasn't sure Alex heard her.

She stared straight ahead as she skated toward Kimmy and Debra. They were still waving and motioning for her to hurry back.

Time to begin, she thought, feeling the heaviness return to her legs, feeling the dull dread weigh on her stomach, feeling the fear tighten her throat.

Time for the moment I've been dreading.

It's party time, Corky thought bitterly.

Debra carried the candlesticks in a shoebox. Kimmy held the old book under one arm. The three girls made their way across the ice, moving away from the others.

The heavy clouds hung even lower over them. From far in the distance they heard the dull honking of geese.

Don't geese go south in the winter? Corky wondered.

No time to think about geese, she scolded herself. Kimmy and Debra moved steadily over the ice, their faces set, their eyes narrow with determination.

Hurrying to keep up with them, Corky glanced back to the shore. Where was Ivy? Corky saw several couples skating arm in arm. She saw Jay doing his crazy dance—arms thrashing and flying above his head—in front of a group of kids.

And there stood Ivy at the edge of the group. Her bright red ski suit glowed like fire in the midst of all the duller colors.

When Corky turned back, Debra was already bending down to spread the candlesticks on the ice. "It's a little protected here," she announced. "Not quite as windy as over there. But you two will still have to help block the wind so I can get the candles lit."

Corky squatted down and helped Debra place the candles in a perfect ring. She kept glancing across the ice at Ivy.

Does Ivy have any idea what we're about to do? Corky wondered. Does she have any idea that we're about to chant words to call spirits forth?

The plan was so simple. Simple and terrifying at the same time.

Light the ring of candles. Chant the words. If the evil is inside Ivy, she will be drawn forward, pulled across the ice to them.

If Ivy is pulled by the chant, Corky and her two friends will know for sure, know that she is the one possessed by the evil.

"We'll hold Ivy down, sit on her if we have to," Kimmy had said when they made their plan in Debra's room. "We'll knock her out. Do anything we have to. Then we'll break through the ice and drown the evil again. Drown poor Ivy."

Ivy had to drown for the evil to leave her body,

Corky knew. Corky knew it *too* well. She had drowned for the same reason, had drowned and been revived once the evil was in the water.

"We'll drown Ivy, then revive her once she's free of the evil, once she's Ivy again."

It had seemed a terrifying plan when they made it. Now, as Debra struggled to light the candles, it seemed even more terrifying to Corky. She felt a wave of panic wash over her, paralyze her, tighten every muscle so that she had to struggle to breathe.

Do we have a choice?

No. Corky answered her own question.

Ivy will kill us all—if we don't drown the evil now.

Corky glanced back across the ice. She saw that Ivy had stepped away from the crowd. She was turned toward Corky and her friends.

Did she suspect? Did she have a feeling they were about to trap her? Was she moving toward them—to stop them?

"Hurry," Corky whispered.

Blown by the wind, a candle flickered out. Debra relit it, the lighter trembling in her hand.

And now the candles were all lit again, their flames leaning first in one direction, then the other. Kimmy handed Debra the old book. Debra turned the pages quickly, held the book open between them, and pointed to the passage.

The three of them were on their knees on the ice, Debra between Corky and Kimmy. She held the book by the spine in one hand, resting it against her legs. Holding a long red candle in her other hand, she lowered it over the candles, slowly circling the ring of fire with it.

"Come forward, spirit!" Debra cried, her eyes on Ivy.

"Come forward, spirit!"

Corky squinted through the deepening gray. Ivy stood by herself, hands at her sides.

Was she watching?

Debra started and the others joined in, chanting in low voices, muffled by the steady brush of the wind. Chanting as Debra slowly, rhythmically, moved the candle over the ring of flames.

Chanting.

Calling the evil spirit forward. Calling it to them.

Their voices grew louder, rising over the wind as they continued to chant. And as they repeated the words, Corky's eyes were locked on Ivy.

Were the words drawing her to them? Was she coming across the ice?

Yes.

Here she comes, Corky saw.

Chapter 15

THE EVIL COMES FORWARD

"Keep chanting," Debra whispered. "Don't stop. It's working."

Corky and her two friends lowered their faces to the book and continued the chant. Their voices were a low murmur against the rush of wind over the ice.

A soft rumbling made Corky glance up.

What was that sound? she wondered.

Thunder?

A candlestick toppled over as the ice began to shake.

Deep cracks spider-webbed over the surface.

"Hey—the ice!" Corky shouted.

The rumbling grew to a roar. The ice trembled, tilted, shook.

Corky heard a *crack*. Like a board breaking.

The candles fell onto their sides. A hard tremor shook the book from Debra's hand. Corky saw the fear on her friends' faces as the ice at their feet split open.

Is it an *earthquake*?

That was Corky's last thought as the roar grew louder, louder—until it drowned out all thinking.

A searing pain shot through her head as the deafening roar rattled her eardrums. She pressed her hands to her ears. And shut her eyes—as the explosion tossed her back.

Blown off her knees, she shot backward. She opened her eyes in time to watch Kimmy and Debra tossed back beside her, tossed by the force of the invisible blast.

Her arms shot up helplessly. She landed hard on her back. Felt the power of the explosion roar over her.

Struggling to breathe, Corky stared as the ice split open farther, rumbling, roaring. A swirling mass of thick black smoke funneled up from beneath the surface.

The smoke rose up, spinning, spinning like a cyclone, and a sour stench filled the air. Corky gasped as the sickening odor swept over her.

She grabbed on to Kimmy and watched in horror as the black smoke whirled up, up from the depths of the river, and swept over the shore.

A malodorous blanket of black fog, it blew over the shocked skaters, over Ivy, standing alone, over Jay and his friends, huddled on the ice, over Heather and Lauren at the cider table.

The sour smoke darkened the ice, blackened the sky. Corky heard the frightened cries of birds as they fluttered off their tree perches, the shrill shriek of the ducks and geese around the river's curve.

The ice blistered and burned. The smoke spewed up thicker, faster, swirling up over the shivering trees, up to the clouds.

"What have we *done?*" Corky cried, still sprawled on the ice clinging to Kimmy.

"The evil—it *wasn't* in Ivy!" Kimmy wailed.

"We were wrong! We were wrong!" Debra shouted over the roaring smoke. "It wasn't in Ivy!"

"Our chant called it up!" Corky realized. "We brought the evil to life! We've *unleashed* it!"

PART TWO

GAME TIME

Chapter 16

THE GAMES BEGIN

"**T**his drawer is stuck," Kimmy groaned, shaking the whole dresser in her attempt to get the drawer open.

"You can use the bottom one," Ivy told her. "It's empty."

"How did you unpack so fast?" Kimmy asked Ivy, bending to pull open the drawer.

"I left a lot of stuff in my bag," Ivy replied, fiddling with her hair in front of the mirror. "You know. Stuff that won't wrinkle." She shook her head. "My hair is totally frizzy. This room is so damp!"

Corky stood at the window, peering out at the pink and blue neon sign over the parking lot. CLIFFSIDE INN. *No acancy*.

"The *V* burned out," she reported.

Kimmy glanced up from down on the floor. "What are you talking about, Corky?"

"The sign," Corky replied absently.

"Can you see a cliff out there?" Ivy demanded, struggling to wrap a rubber band around her bushy hair. "Isn't there supposed to be a cliff?"

"All I can see is the parking lot," Corky reported. "And the highway."

"There is supposed to be a cliff. And a really pretty lake," Kimmy told them. "My parents have been to New Foster."

"I think Debra, Heather, and Lauren's room is on the other side of the motel," Corky said, watching two large yellow Ryder trucks roar by on the highway. "We'll have to check it out. Maybe they have scenery from their window."

"Does the TV work?" Kimmy asked. She shoved the bottom drawer shut and climbed to her feet. "There. All unpacked."

"Who has time for TV?" Ivy replied, still struggling with her long hair. "The bus will be here to take us to the arena in a few minutes."

"I can't believe the team isn't staying here!" Corky moaned.

Kimmy snickered. "I guess you and Alex had big plans, huh? If Ms. Closter catches you . . ."

Corky felt her face growing hot. "Shut up, Kimmy!" she replied, laughing. She picked up a hairbrush from the bed and heaved it at Kimmy.

Kimmy ducked and the hairbrush smashed against the dresser.

"Oh. Can I use that? I forgot mine," Ivy said.

"Sure. Go ahead," Corky told her.

Ever since the skating party at the river a few days before, Corky and Kimmy had been extra nice to Ivy. All because of guilt, Corky realized. How could we have misjudged Ivy like that? she asked herself. How could we have accused Ivy of those terrible accidents?

Ivy had been innocent, the three girls now knew. Ivy had *not* been possessed by the evil.

Corky and her friends hadn't mentioned the evil at all. None of them wanted to talk about it. Or think about what they had done. It was all too scary. Instead, they had spent the time concentrating on their routines, preparing for the Holiday Tournament at New Foster.

A busy but peaceful time, Corky thought gratefully.

No sign of the evil. No accidents. No frightening surprises.

Maybe the evil blew away, Corky thought hopefully, gazing out the window. Maybe it swept right past everyone at the party and kept on going.

"The team is staying right down the road," Ivy reported. "The New Foster Motor Lodge. We passed it on our way here. The arena is right behind it, remember?"

"It looked even tackier than this place!" Kimmy commented, pulling on the top of her uniform and tugging down the sleeves.

"Stop complaining, Kimmy!" Corky scolded. "We're away from home, right? We're going to do our routines in front of hundreds of people. And we're going to win the basketball tournament!"

"Go Tigers!" All three girls shouted enthusiastically.

Laughing, they burst into the Hoop cheer.

Later they hurried out front to get on the bus, laughing and singing. Corky relaxed and gave in to the excitement of being away at a tournament. She had a feeling that everything was going to be okay.

> Everything is okay,
> Shadyside has come to play!
> Everything is okay,
> Shadyside is on its way!
> Everything is okay,
> Shadyside is going to WIN!

Corky and the five other cheerleaders finished the cheer in a wavelike ripple, dropping down into splits one after the other. They jumped to their feet and trotted to the sidelines waving red and white pom-poms above their heads as the Tigers band broke into a march.

Corky glanced down the line of happy, excited girls. Even Debra, normally so cool and aloof, was flushed, her blue eyes wide with excitement.

"You kept hitting me with your pom-pom!" Corky

told Heather, shouting over the crowd. "You're dangerous!"

Heather laughed. "Sorry! I was staring up at the crowd. I didn't realize!"

The New Foster Arena was much bigger than Corky had imagined. The lights made the polished hardwood floor glow like glass. The red plastic seats appeared to rise straight up to the ceiling. And tonight, most of the seats were filled even though it was only the first game of the first round of the tournament.

The Billingham Lions cheerleaders—all ten of them!—were on the floor now, performing a rap routine. The crowd really got into it, Corky saw, watching from beside the Tigers' bench. Billingham was just a few miles from New Foster. A lot of Lions fans had shown up.

Tigers versus the Lions, Corky thought. It's perfect.

One cheerleader on the Lions' squad really stood out. She was tall and well built and very athletic, with long black hair that fell to her waist and a pale, pretty face with big green eyes. Dramatic eyes.

"That's Lena," Debra said, leaning close to Corky to be heard. "That girl you're staring at. Her name is Lena something-or-other. She's good, isn't she? I remember her from cheerleader camp last year."

Corky didn't have time to reply. It was almost time for the teams to be introduced. Time for one last pregame cheer.

Tigers, let's score!
Two points, then more!
[stomp stomp]
Tigers, let's score!
Two points, then more!
[stomp stomp]

"Louder! I can't hear you!" Kimmy shouted.

Tigers, let's score!
Two points, then more!
[stomp stomp]

"Louder! I still can't hear you!"

The crowd roared and stomped as the girls repeated the chant louder and louder. They ended with tuck jumps and trotted off the floor.

"That was great!" Corky cried breathlessly.

"Down! Everybody down!" Kimmy instructed.

They knelt on one knee as the teams came running onto the floor to be introduced. Alex flashed Corky a thumbs-up as he jogged past. Jay, following right behind Alex, had a wide, goofy grin on his face.

The players on both teams picked up basketballs and began warming up, dribbling back and forth, passing, shooting layups and jump shots. Alex and Jay were laughing about something, Corky saw. They both seemed really loose.

Why does it seem I'm more nervous than they are? she asked herself.

She hadn't felt this excited in a long time. The lights reflecting off the polished floor, the shouts of the crowd, the thud of basketballs—all made her feel happy.

"Go TIGERS!" she shouted, jumping up and down, barely able to contain her energy.

The game got off to a good start. Alex jumped and tipped the ball to Gary Brandt, who took it in for an easy layup under the basket.

> Tigers, let's score!
> Two points, then more!
> [stomp stomp]

It was two to nothing. As the half progressed, the Tigers never lost the lead.

With less than two minutes in the half, the Lions tied the game with a three-point shot by their center. The crowd went wild, roaring and stomping until the entire arena shook.

As a Tigers' time-out was called, Corky watched Lena, the Lions cheerleader, rush out on the floor. Lena performed three perfect handsprings, her long black hair flying as she moved.

Wow! Corky thought. She's awesome!

Corky had always been a talented cheerleader. Before they moved to Shadyside, Corky and her sister Bobbi had led their squad from St. Louis to the ESPN cheerleading championships.

But Corky had never seen a cheerleader as graceful *and* athletic as Lena.

"Couldn't you just *kill* her?" Lauren declared.

Corky laughed. She dropped to one knee beside

Lauren as the buzzer went off and the game continued. "Go TIGERS!"

Jay passed the ball in to Alex. Alex dribbled downcourt, almost lost the dribble, spun around, recovered, and passed it back to Jay. Jay moved under the net, pulled up as if to shoot—but passed it back to Alex at the foul stripe. Alex sank an easy jump shot.

The Tigers regained the lead and kept it. As the teams trotted off at halftime, both bands blaring, the scoreboard read TIGERS 44, LIONS 34.

"Confetti cannons! *Move,* everyone!" Ms. Closter was shouting, cupping her hands around her mouth. "Confetti cannons! Let's go!"

Corky glanced back reluctantly as the three cannons were rolled onto the floor.

"It's okay," Lauren assured her, placing a hand on Corky's shoulder. She must have caught the doubtful expression on Corky's face. "Ivy and I checked them out before the game. No problem this time."

"Aim them toward the Shadyside section! Up there!" Ms. Closter instructed, pointing.

"Okay, everyone! Let's make the handsprings perfect!" Kimmy shouted. "Let's show Lena she isn't the only one who can do them!"

Corky took her place in line behind the cannons. The cannons were drawing a lot of attention. Corky could see kids pointing to them, asking one another about them.

She was so busy staring up at the crowd, she nearly missed the start of the cheer.

> HOOP—there it is!
> HOOP—there it is!
> HOOP—there it is!
> TWO POINTS!

As the chant continued, the crowd picked it up, clapping and stomping. Again, the arena felt as if it were going to shake to the ground.

Corky stepped up to the cannon as the three cheerleaders began their handsprings. She grabbed the cord and prepared to trigger her cannon.

All three cheerleaders were ready, she saw.

She pulled the cord and raised her eyes to the crowd, waiting for the colorful blast of confetti to fly over them.

The wet gurgling sound startled her.

It was so bright out on the arena floor, so hard to see.

Corky didn't realize how horribly wrong it all was until the cries and screams from the stands pierced her ears.

"It's *burning!*"

"Look out!"

"Ooooh—it stinks!"

"Stop it! Somebody *stop* it!"

She lowered her gaze to see geysers of steaming black tar spewing up from all three cannons.

The thick black tar rose high in the air, then splashed down over the seats with a loud *smacking* sound.

Spectators shoved toward the aisles to get out of the way. Angry cries and screams rose.

"Make them stop! Make them stop!" Lauren was shrieking.

But the boiling tar continued to spew out of the cannons.

I know who did this, Corky thought, holding her nose to try to shut out the foul stench.

I know who did this.

Chapter 17

WHO IS IT?

"The evil did this. It's all our fault." Corky whispered, *"We* brought the evil back."

"I know," Debra whispered back. "But the evil has to inhabit someone. Who is it? Is it one of us? Someone who was at the skating party? We've *got* to find out."

The six cheerleaders were huddled on a bench in the girls' locker room in the basement of the arena. Upstairs the arena staff was struggling to clean up the mess. Police officers were investigating, questioning anyone who might have had an opportunity to rig the cannons.

Ivy leaned against a metal locker, her eyes shut,

frowning. Lauren hovered over her friend, trying to comfort her. Lauren's skirt had a black stain down one side.

Heather sat hunched over on the bench, her head resting in her hands, staring down at the floor. Kimmy sat beside her, her cheeks bright red, her black hair matted to her wet forehead.

At the end of the bench, facing the locker room door, Corky and Debra whispered their fears to each other. The room smelled of sweat. The air hung heavy and wet. Somewhere on the other side of the lockers, water dripped. A steady *drip, drip, drip.*

"Since when do you chew your nails?" Debra whispered.

Corky lowered her hand. "I—I didn't realize I was doing it," she confessed. She gazed down at her finger. To her surprise, she had chewed the skin beneath the nail until it bled.

"What a disgusting mess," Debra murmured. "They'll never get the tar cleaned up. Does everyone blame us?"

"I don't know." Corky's voice caught in her throat. She felt so disappointed, so guilty. This was supposed to be an exciting night. Not a night of horror.

The locker room door swung open, and Ms. Closter entered, her features set, her eyes narrowed. She wore her usual oversize white T-shirt over a pair of black leggings.

She stepped up to the cheerleaders, shaking her head. Corky saw that her eyes were watery and red rimmed. "Miraculously not one person was seriously hurt," she reported grimly.

Ivy let out a loud sob.

She's acting so upset, Corky thought suspiciously. Isn't she overdoing it a little?

"Do any of you know *anything* about this?" the adviser demanded, her eyes moving slowly down the row of girls. "Anything at all?"

"Ivy and I checked the cannons this evening," Lauren offered, her arm around Ivy's trembling shoulders. "They were fine. They were filled with confetti."

"Did any of you see *anyone* hanging around them before the game?" Ms. Closter asked. "Did anyone see anything suspicious at all?"

No one replied.

Corky lowered her eyes to the floor.

"This is a horrible, horrible prank that some sick individual played," Ms. Closter said heatedly. "Some very sick individual. My guess is that someone on the Lions, or some Lions supporter, rigged the cannons as a practical joke."

She sighed. "Some joke," she muttered bitterly.

The locker room door swung open. The basketball coach stuck his head in. He was a young man, younger than Ms. Closter, but his brown hair was thinning on top. He was short, kind of chubby, with a round, friendly face.

He usually flashed a warm smile to everyone. But as Corky raised her eyes to the doorway, she saw that his expression was grim. "Obviously we can't finish the game tonight," he reported to Ms. Closter. "We're going to try to squeeze it in at noon tomorrow. Before the regularly scheduled game. If they can get the seats cleaned up."

Ms. Closter nodded, her expression as grim as the coach's.

"Anybody see anyone messing with the cannons?" the coach asked her.

Ms. Closter shook her head. "We haven't a clue."

Yes, we do, Corky thought bitterly. We *do* have a clue. It wasn't a little practical joke pulled by a Lions' supporter. I know that for sure, Corky told herself.

It was a trick played by an evil spirit hundreds of years old. An evil spirit that *we* called back.

And this evil spirit may be in this room right now, may even be sitting on this bench.

Corky jumped to her feet, unable to stop the chills that swept down her back one after another.

She dreamed about the evil that night.

In the dream she couldn't see it, but she knew it was there.

She could sense it in the swirl of gray smoke that curled up in the strange, white-walled room where she stood. She backed up, frightened, alert to its presence, pressing her spine against the white wall.

The wall was cold. So cold.

The gray smoke curled around her.

Kimmy and Debra appeared in the room. They kept

yelling at Corky, yelling frantically. They pointed accusingly at her, the two of them, shouting and pointing their fingers together.

What are they saying? Corky wondered. Why are they pointing at me? Why can't I understand them?

Because it's a dream, she told herself.

And as soon as she realized she was dreaming, she woke up. Gazed around the dark room. Didn't know where she was.

It took Corky a few seconds to remember she was in a motel room in New Foster. Peering across the dark room, she could see Kimmy and Ivy in the double bed against the wall.

Pink and blue neon light from the sign out front spilled in through the window, onto their bed. Ivy snored lightly. Kimmy slept on the far edge of the bed, her back to Ivy.

Corky jumped when she heard the tap on the window.

Two taps. A pause. Then three taps, a little harder.

She realized at once that someone was out there. Someone was tapping on her window.

Her dream still fresh in her mind, Corky lowered her feet to the floor.

Tap tap. Tap tap tap.

Whoever is tapping on the window is the *evil!*

The evil has come for me, Corky thought, feeling the goose bumps rise on both arms. *Whoever is tapping on the window is the evil!*

I know it. I know it for sure.

Tap tap tap. Tap tap. Even louder.

Corky took a deep breath. Then she crept to the window and peered out.

Who is it? Who's out there?

When she saw the face behind the glass, Corky let out a startled cry.

Chapter 18

THE EVIL EYE

*H*er heart pounding, Corky pulled up the window. "Alex—what are you doing here?" she whispered, unable to hide her shock.

He shrugged. He had a black and gray Raiders cap pulled over his blond hair. His Shadyside High jacket was unsnapped, revealing an olive-green pullover. The neon light fell over his face, making his grin appear eerie, unnatural.

"How did you get here?" Corky demanded, glancing back to make sure Ivy and Kimmy hadn't awakened.

"Walked," he replied. His breath steamed up pink and blue in the strange light of the motel parking lot.

121

"All the way from your motel?" Corky sounded surprised. "Why?"

"I couldn't sleep," he replied. "Come on out. It's not too cold."

"Huh?" She stared out at him, studying his face, trying to decide what to do.

"Let's take a walk," he urged. "A short walk. It's not too cold. Really. I—I'm just too pumped to sleep."

A gust of cold wind fluttered the drapes. "But I'm not dressed!" Corky whispered.

Alex laughed. "Hurry. Just throw something on. It's nice out. Really."

Corky backed away from the window. In the darkness, she pulled on a sweatshirt and the jeans she had worn earlier. *If we get caught, we'll be in major trouble,* she thought.

She grabbed her jacket, then stepped back to the window. She had a feeling that Alex would no longer be there, that he might have vanished, like her dream.

But there he was with his hands in his jacket pockets, staring up at the motel sign. When he saw Corky, he turned quickly and helped her out of the window. He held her waist tightly as she lowered herself to the ground.

"You're bad," she whispered, flashing him a teasing grin.

"I'm totally wired," he said. "There was no way I could get to sleep. I mean, the game was going so great. We were going to win. I could just feel it. I was so pumped!"

She placed a hand on his sleeve and led him away from the window. They made their way slowly around the side of the one-story green stucco motel.

"And then that thing with the cannons!" Alex continued, talking rapidly, excitedly. "What was *that* about? I mean, that was really weird!"

"It was horrible," Corky muttered, leaning against him as they walked. "So totally gross."

"And when I realized we couldn't play the second half, I—I just about freaked!" Alex continued. He shook his head. "I just couldn't calm down enough to get to sleep."

He turned and slid his arms under her jacket, around her waist. His blue eyes locked on hers as he lowered his head to kiss her.

But Corky gently pushed him away. "Whoa. I want to talk first."

His expression turned to one of surprise. "Talk? What about?"

"About you," Corky replied, working up her courage. "How come you've been so weird lately?" It was time to have it out with him, Corky decided. It was time to hear the truth. If he wanted to break up with her, he shouldn't be calling her out of her room in the middle of the night, acting so romantic.

"Me? Weird?" he asked innocently. He pulled off the Raiders cap and scratched his head. Then he shoved the cap back on.

"You've been very strange lately," Corky insisted. She squeezed his hand. "Showing up late. Or not showing up at all. Giving me lame excuses." She

123

raised her eyes to his as if searching for answers there. "It's time to tell me the truth, Alex. What is your problem? What's going on?"

He took a step back, letting go of Corky's hand. "Okay, okay. You're right," he replied solemnly. "I'll tell you. I guess I should've told you weeks ago. When it started. But—"

"When *what* started?" Corky demanded, feeling her throat tighten.

Alex hesitated. He avoided her stare. "I got a tutor," he murmured.

Corky wasn't sure she had heard correctly. "You— what?"

"I had to get a tutor," Alex repeated reluctantly. "A tutor for math. I'm supposed to be the class brain— right? But—well— I guess the pressure got to me or something. I got behind and couldn't catch up. So my parents got me a tutor. But it's embarrassing. Really. I didn't want anyone to know, so—"

Corky's mouth dropped open. "All those times I called, and you couldn't come to the phone? All those nights you didn't want to come over and study together?"

"It was because I had to go to my tutor," Alex replied, still avoiding her eyes.

Corky felt like laughing out loud. But somehow she managed to hold it in. "I don't *believe* you!" she told him, rolling her eyes. "You are such an egotist! Did you really think kids would get on your case be- cause—"

"Don't make fun of me," he said sharply.

A truck roared by on the highway. The wind grew colder, damper. With a shiver, Corky took Alex's arm and they started walking again, circling the motel parking lot.

"You could've told me," Corky scolded softly. "You know you can trust me, Alex."

He stopped near the front of the building and turned to her. "I was just too embarrased, I guess," he said. Then he pulled her close and kissed her.

His kiss was soft at first, then harder, hungrier.

He seems different, Corky thought. His kiss is different.

He suddenly seems so—needy.

Gripping her tightly, Alex backed Corky against the building as he pressed his mouth against hers.

Glancing over his shoulder, Corky saw a figure come into focus at the corner of the building.

Saw a familiar face. Staring at them.

Jay!

Why was he just standing there, staring like that?

As Corky gazed back at him, she saw Jay's eyes glow red, an angry, evil red. Animal eyes. Inhuman eyes.

Or was it just the glare from the neon sign?

Corky pushed Alex back. "Alex—look." She started to point to Jay.

He was gone.

Chapter 19

LENA FLIPS

When Corky and the other cheerleaders arrived at the arena at ten-thirty the next morning, the basketball players were already on the floor.

"Energy up! Energy up!" the coach was shouting. He made a sweeping motion with both hands. "Two laps for everyone! Let's go! Get those hearts beating!"

Several players groaned. But they all obediently began jogging along the sidelines.

"Energy up! Energy up!" the coach repeated, turning in place in the center of the floor, studying the team as they trotted by.

"They look half dead," Kimmy muttered to Corky as they stepped onto the floor. Kimmy dropped the box of red and white pom-poms onto the bench.

126

"They don't look too awake," Corky agreed, thinking about Alex's surprise visit the night before. And once again picturing Jay's strange, frightening stare. "They were psyched last night. It's too bad they couldn't finish the game then."

Kimmy nodded, then hurried over to give Heather and Lauren some last-minute instructions.

As the players approached, jogging at a steady clip, Corky took a few steps onto the floor and tried to get Jay's attention. "Hey, Jay! Jay?"

He jogged right past. He didn't seem to hear her.

Corky wanted to ask him why he hadn't said hi the night before. It wasn't like Jay, she knew. He wasn't at all shy. He never cared if he interrupted Alex and her.

"Two's company, three's a party!" That's what Jay always said.

So what was his problem last night? Corky wondered. Thinking about his strange, glowing eyes gave Corky a chill.

Alex hadn't seemed the same either. His kisses were so much rougher, so much harder.

Am I imagining that Alex and Jay seem different? Corky asked herself. Is it just me? Just the fact that I'm uncomfortable being in this strange town— knowing that the evil may have followed us here?

She glanced up at the section of seats that had been covered in the boiling tar. Most of the tar had been cleaned up. But many seats were still stained with black marks.

Stop it, Corky! she scolded herself.

I'm not going to think about that today. No way. We

have a game to win. I'm going to concentrate on the game. I'm going to concentrate on having fun.

The players finished their second lap, picked up basketballs, and began their regular warm-ups. Across the floor, Corky saw the Lions cheerleaders come running out of their locker room in their blue and gold uniforms.

Her sleek black hair drifting behind her, Lena lowered her hands to the bench and began doing stretching exercises. She is really beautiful, Corky thought. And look how limber she is. Wow!

"I hate her. I really hate her."

Corky turned to find Ivy standing behind her, arms crossed tightly over her chest, a disapproving frown on her face as she stared across the floor at Lena. Lauren hurried over to join them.

Corky laughed. "Why do you hate Lena, Ivy? Because she's pretty and a really great cheerleader?"

"That's good for starters," Ivy replied dryly. "I just hate that girl. She's such a show-off. I mean, she really thinks she's a star."

As if responding to Ivy's words, Lena stepped onto the floor and started performing back flips.

Perfect each time, Corky observed.

"I hate her!" Ivy repeated.

Lena finished her back flips and smiled across the court at Corky and Ivy. "Go Lions!" she shouted as if challenging them.

"Go Tigers!" Ivy and Lauren shouted back.

Corky bent to retie her sneaker lace. A loud, angry shout on the court made her raise her head.

"Get out of my face!" Jay screamed at the coach.

Corky saw the startled expression on the man's face. "Hey, Landers—I only said to pick it up a little!"

Jay's face had become bright red. His eyes glowed angrily. "You've been riding me all morning!" he screamed. He furiously tossed his basketball to the side. It hit a metal folding chair and sent it clattering to the floor. "Get out of my face! I mean it!"

"Hey—cool your jets, Jay. Let's talk about this!" Coach Hall replied, motioning with both hands for Jay to back off and calm down. He put his hand on Jay's back and started to lead him off the floor.

"Get your paws *off* me!" Jay shrieked. He pulled away from the coach and went running off the floor toward the locker rooms.

Coach Hall, shaking his head, went after him.

I've never seen Jay like this, Corky thought, swallowing hard. What is his *problem?*

She caught Alex's eye. He shrugged, a bewildered expression on his face. "I guess he had a bad breakfast!" he shouted to her.

Corky glanced up at the scoreboard clock. Eleven o'clock. The second half of the game against the Lions would begin in an hour. A few early-bird fans were already making their way up the aisles to their seats.

> We're the best,
> Better than the rest!
> We're the best,
> Better than the rest!

Corky turned to see that an impromptu cheerleader competition had begun. Lena and the other Lions cheerleaders had lined up and offered a challenge across the floor.

Kimmy quickly called the Tigers into a huddle. Then they lined up to answer the challenge.

> We're the Tigers
> And all we have to say
> is: We're the BEST
> In every way!
> We're the Tigers
> And all we have to say
> is: Look out, Lions—
> Tigers are on their way!

Corky and her teammates ended with a shout. Then they watched Lena call instructions to the Lions, who stepped forward to answer the Tiger challenge.

> Two points more AND
> Two points more AND
> Two points more AND
> Two points more AND—

Each time the cheerleaders called out *And,* Lena performed a crisp, clean backflip.

Corky watched in total admiration. Lena had to be the best cheerleader Corky had ever seen.

Two points more AND
Two points more AND
Two points more AND
Two points more AND—
WINNNNNNN, LIONS!

As the Lions cheerleaders clapped, Lena did another backflip, landing perfectly on her feet. Then another backflip.

Then, even though the cheer had ended, she stood straight, swung her arms up, and performed another backflip, her long hair flying.

"Do you *believe* her?" Kimmy whispered to Corky.

Another backflip. Another. The basketball players had all stopped their warm-ups to watch.

Another backflip.

And then Lena's trembling voice rang out over the court. "Somebody—help me!"

Another backflip.

Corky watched the terror on Lena's face as she flipped again.

"Help me! *Please!* I can't stop!"

Chapter 20

A BIG DRINK

*T*wo Lions cheerleaders grabbed for Lena. But she flipped away from them, her black hair flying, her long legs stretching up together, her sneakers landing hard.

Hoarse screams escaped her throat. Her eyes rolled wildly as she performed another backflip. Then another.

Alarmed voices rang out as players and cheerleaders from both schools hurried across the floor.

"Grab her!"

"Somebody hold her down!"

"Why is she doing that?"

"Make her stop!"

"Why is she screaming?"

Three basketball players finally pinned Lena to the

floor. Her arms shot forward. Her legs kicked as if going into a flip. As the three boys struggled to hold her down, Lena tossed her head back—her eyes rolling around frantically—and uttered scream after scream.

Corky saw the Lions coach run toward the phones along the back wall, probably to call for an ambulance. A crowd of players, cheerleaders, and onlookers formed a circle around Lena. They talked softly, shaking their heads in disbelief as Lena thrashed her arms and legs, trying hard to break free to perform more backflips.

"Noooo!"

Several kids cried out as Lena hurtled away from her captors. She tossed her hair back, raised her hands high, and did another arching backflip.

Then another.

As she flipped herself over, her shrill screams pierced the air.

"Stop her! Somebody stop her!" Corky shrieked. Glancing back, she saw Ivy, hanging back, away from the circle of horrified onlookers, arms casually crossed over her chest.

"Hey!" Corky cried out in dismay as she saw the pleased grin frozen on Ivy's face.

"We won!" Ivy cried happily, jumping up and down.

"Glad this one is over!" Kimmy muttered to Corky, wiping sweat off her forehead with the back of her hand.

Me too, Corky thought with a sigh.

The Tigers won the game easily. It was a low-scoring low-energy half, Corky had to admit. The band tried extra hard to get everyone clapping and cheering. But the cheerleaders on both sides couldn't get into the game.

They were all too shaken by what had happened to Lena.

Corky couldn't erase the sound of Lena's terrified screams from her mind. She couldn't forget that she and Kimmy and Debra had called the evil back. The sight of Lena struggling, struggling with all her might to free herself as the medics strapped her down to a gurney and rolled her to the ambulance stayed in Corky's mind.

No one had recovered from that sight yet.

During the game spectators milled around, talking, not paying much attention.

Alex played his usual strong game. He was the top scorer of both teams. But Corky could see the strained, tight-lipped expression on his face, even after he scored a basket.

And she knew Alex *had* to be unhappy that Jay wasn't in the game.

Jay sat glumly on the bench, resting his head in his hands, watching the play move from one end to the other. Corky guessed that the coach had benched him because of his outburst before the game.

What a shame, Corky thought. Jay is usually the team cheerleader, calling out encouragement to the others, shouting wisecracks, slapping high-fives after every play.

But not today. Today he sat on the far end of the bench, staring unhappily at the game, not moving, not smiling, not talking to anyone.

"On to the second round!" Ms. Closter shouted. "Hope you girls have some voice left! I'm so hoarse! My throat is *killing* me!"

The cheerleaders and both teams headed off the floor. Corky and Debra found themselves leading the way to the back hall that led to their locker rooms.

"Corky, we have to talk," Debra said, staring meaningfully into Corky's eyes. "What happened to Lena —it could be caused by only one thing."

"I know," Corky replied. She pushed through the swinging doors. Into the outer hallway.

She stopped when she saw the body sprawled on its back across the concrete floor. "Noooo!" A horrified wail escaped Corky's mouth.

Debra grabbed her arm, squeezing hard. "I—don't believe it!"

Corky heard startled cries behind her as cheerleaders and players jammed into the narrow hall to see what had happened.

She shrank back, Debra still squeezing her arm, and stared down at the grotesque form on the floor.

The Tigers coach lay with his arms stretched out. The neck of an enormous green water bottle from a cooler had been shoved into his mouth.

The huge bottle rested on his face. Empty.

The water had all drained out into his body, Corky saw.

The coach had drowned. His belly and chest were bloated. Like a big water balloon.

What have we done? Corky thought, turning her head away. What have we done?

She heard cries and moans all around her.

Debra leaned close. Her voice trembled as she murmured in Corky's ear. "The evil—it's right here. Right here beside us now."

Chapter 21

OUT THE WINDOW

"We're going to win this tournament for Coach Hall!" Alex cried, raising a fist in the air.

Several kids let out a cheer. But the response was halfhearted, Corky saw. Three hours later they were all still dazed and upset. The shock hadn't begun to wear off. Both players and cheerleaders remained silent, still deep in their own troubled thoughts.

"We're not going to let this stop the Tigers!" Alex continued, trying to rouse them. "The police will find the killer. And we're going to show everyone that we're not quitters!"

Sweat dripped down Alex's face. His thick blond hair was matted to his forehead. His eyes flashed wildly, excitedly.

Corky glanced around the dimly lit locker room. Her friends huddled in twos and threes, some leaning against the gray lockers, some hunched close together on the low benches.

The blue-uniformed New Foster police officers had questioned each of them. Two officers were still questioning Ms. Closter near the locker room doorway.

Upstairs, Coach Hall's bloated body lay sprawled on its back as officers searched the arena for clues. Corky wondered if they had removed the water bottle from his mouth.

It's so sick, so *sick,* she thought, forcing back a wave of nausea. She leaned close to Kimmy. "I just want to go home," she whispered.

Kimmy's eyes were red rimmed and bloodshot. She slumped on the bench beside Corky, her face pale and expressionless. "Me too," she whispered back.

Corky overheard two basketball players murmuring to each other against the wall behind her. "Who would kill the coach? He was such a good guy."

"It had to be someone really strong."

"Yeah. Those water bottles weigh a ton!"

"It had to be a psycho. A total psycho."

Corky swallowed hard. The killer wasn't human, she knew. The killer had inhuman strength because he—or she—was inhabited by the evil.

Forcing back the dread that made her stomach turn and rumble, Corky gazed around the room at the dazed faces.

Only Alex seemed to have shaken away his shock. He continued to deliver his emotional pep talk, thrusting his fist above his head, his blue eyes wild, his voice hoarse and breathless.

Why is Alex *doing* this? Corky wondered, studying him as he shouted. He tried to rouse the others to cheer with him. How did he get over his shock so quickly?

And then her eyes stopped on Jay.

Jay stood beside Alex, one foot on the low bench in front of him, his Mighty Ducks cap pulled low on his forehead, a white towel wrapped around his neck.

Corky gasped as she realized Jay was staring back at her. His eyes were narrowed, his expression cold and hard.

"Kimmy, do you see Jay?" she whispered. "Why is he staring like that?"

"Maybe he's just upset," Kimmy replied, raising her eyes to the front of the locker room, where Jay continued to stare, unblinking, unmoving. "Maybe he's just as frightened as the rest of us."

"But why does Jay look so different? He doesn't look like Jay at all," Corky insisted. "He—he's really scaring me."

"We're all scared," Kimmy replied softly, lowering her eyes to the floor."

Corky remembered how angry Jay had been before the game.

"You don't think that Jay—" she started to say.

Kimmy interrupted her. "We just have to get home, Corky. We have to get away from here. Before we all die."

* * *

The police didn't allow them to leave the arena until evening. After one set of officers questioned them, another set appeared.

After stopping for dinner at a fast-food place in town, the cheerleaders wearily made their way to their rooms.

"Too late to call home," Corky whispered to Kimmy. "My parents wouldn't drive up here this late."

Kimmy glanced at the bathroom, where Ivy was taking a shower. "We'll wake up early and call," she said. "Did you tell Debra?"

Corky nodded. "Debra wanted to run away—tonight. Just leave all our stuff and try to hitch a ride home."

"That's crazy," Kimmy replied, frowning. "We'll be safe till morning. Then we'll call our parents to come get us."

"But what about all the others?" Corky whispered, pulling on her long nightshirt. "Shouldn't we warn them too?"

"Would they believe us?" Kimmy demanded. "If we told them there was an evil spirit here, would any of them believe us?"

Corky stared back at Kimmy thoughtfully. "No. I guess not," she replied finally.

A chill ran down her back. She could feel the goose bumps rise on her arms. She climbed into bed, shivering, and pulled the blankets up to her chin. "I guess not," she repeated.

The bathroom door swung open, and Ivy emerged,

stepping out of a cloud of steam, one towel wrapped around her body, another around her hair. "I feel much better," she announced. "Much, much better."

Corky couldn't sleep.

She had the shivers and couldn't get warm enough to stop them. Staring up at the ceiling, she listened to trucks rumble by out on the highway—and she pictured the horrors at the arena again and again.

Closing her eyes didn't make them go away. She still saw poor Lena, her face twisted in horror as she did backflip after backflip, unable to stop, unable to control her own body.

She heard Lena's helpless shrieks. They repeated and repeated in Corky's head until Corky covered her ears with both hands.

She saw Jay's angry outburst. Saw him shout at Coach Hall, heave the basketball into the seats. So strange for someone so laid-back, so good-natured.

She saw Coach Hall lying bloated and beached on the hallway floor with the huge green water bottle jammed in his mouth and down his throat.

She couldn't stop these scenes. She couldn't force them away. It was, she realized, as if *she* had been possessed, possessed by these pictures of horror.

Desperate for sleep, Corky shut her eyes and tried to count sheep, silent white sheep.

But a sound from across the room made the sheep vanish.

Corky opened her eyes and gazed through the darkness to see someone moving. Ivy. In the shimmering pink and blue light from the parking lot, Corky watched Ivy pull on a sweater and jeans.

Adjusting the sweater sleeves, Ivy turned toward Corky's bed. Corky instantly shut her eyes, pretended to sleep. A few moments later she opened them again.

Moving silently, with quick, eager movements, Ivy pulled on her shoes, brushed out her long hair, stepped to the window.

Corky raised her head from the pillow to watch.

It must be about four in the morning, she realized. What is going on? Why is Ivy sneaking out?

The window slid open.

Corky sat up a little straighter, squinting into the pink and blue light.

Silently, Ivy raised one leg over the windowsill. Then she leaned forward, pulled up the other leg, and disappeared out the window.

Corky lowered her feet to the floor. "Kimmy?" she called, her voice a hoarse whisper. "Kimmy—did you see that? Ivy sneaked out."

Silence. Kimmy didn't move.

"Kimmy?" Corky called a little louder. "Kimmy?"

Chapter 22

SOMETHING WEIRD

"Kimmy?" Corky called weakly, feeling dread in her chest. She crossed the room to Kimmy's bed. "Kimmy?"

Kimmy finally stirred. "Huh? Corky—what *time* is it?" she asked in a sleep-choked whisper.

"I—I don't know," Corky stammered. "But something weird is going on. Wake up. Ivy just sneaked out the window."

Kimmy sat up and lowered her feet to the floor. "She *what?*"

Corky grabbed Kimmy's hands and pulled her to her feet. "Hurry. Get dressed. We've got to follow her."

Kimmy shook her head as if trying to shake away

her sleepiness. "I don't believe this," she muttered. She clicked on the bedside lamp and began pulling on the jeans and sweatshirt she had tossed on the chair.

A few seconds later both girls were dressed with their jackets on. Corky led the way out the window.

Under the glare of the neon sign, she could see two parked vans and a small car. No cars or trucks moved on the highway. Nothing.

No sign of Ivy.

"This is crazy," Kimmy murmured, pulling her jacket closed as she stepped up beside Corky. "Maybe she's just meeting some guy." Her breath steamed up in front of her as she spoke.

"I don't think so," Corky whispered, her eyes searching the darkness. "Ivy's not very good at keeping secrets. She would've told us."

Corky shivered. Such a cold night, she thought. She found a wool hat in the pocket of her jacket and pulled it on.

Keeping to the deep shadows, she led the way around to the far side of the motel. She stopped and pressed her back to the wall, when she heard voices up ahead.

Familiar voices.

Kimmy grabbed on to Corky's coat sleeve. "Who is it?"

They both leaned forward, squinting into the parking lot.

Corky recognized Ivy first. She stood in front of a black Jeep, pulling her long hair back over the collar of her coat with both hands.

She was talking excitedly to Heather and Lauren.

Corky felt a chill that made her entire body shudder. Even in the darkness of the parking lot, she could see the strange expressions on their faces. Eager, excited faces.

Excited about *what*?

If some kind of secret meeting was planned, why weren't Kimmy and I invited? Corky wondered.

Then she saw figures moving at the side of the Jeep. Alex and Jay stepped into view, followed by six other players on the team.

"They're all here," Corky whispered, hanging back in the shadows. "The whole team."

The players greeted the three cheerleaders. All of them seemed to be talking at once. Corky strained to hear what they were saying. But their hushed voices didn't carry on the still night air.

"They all seem really pumped," Kimmy whispered.

"This is so weird," Corky replied. She saw Alex slap Jay a high-five. One of the guys playfully tugged Ivy's hair. Heather and Lauren were moving their arms in unison. They seemed to be performing a whispered cheer. Two of the players were wrestling with a third.

Then, as if they had been given a signal, they all stopped talking and kidding around. Corky watched their expressions become solemn. They all turned and made their way off the parking lot and into the woods beyond it:

"Should we follow them?" Kimmy asked, still whispering even though the others had left.

Corky hesitated. Where could they be going?

"Those woods lead down to a lake," Kimmy said, stepping away from the building, her eyes narrowed on the black trees beyond the parking lot. "Do you think that's where they're going? Do you think they're having some kind of party, and they didn't invite us because we're the captains?"

"That doesn't make sense," Corky replied. "Maybe you and I should—"

She stopped when she heard rapid footsteps on the pavement behind them.

She gasped. "Kimmy—someone is coming!"

They both spun around.

146

Chapter 23

THE EVIL IS REVEALED

"**D**ebra!" Corky cried.

Debra came trotting up to them, her breath rising in rapid puffs, her cold blue eyes locked on Corky. Her down vest was open, over a dark purple sweater that came down nearly to the knees of her jeans. Her normally perfect blond hair was unbrushed.

"Debra—what are *you* doing here?" Kimmy demanded shrilly.

"Are you going with them?" Corky pointed toward the woods.

"Huh? Going where?" Debra was confused. "I don't get it. You and Kimmy—why are you out here?"

"I asked you first!" Kimmy replied sharply.

"I heard Heather and Lauren get up," Debra explained. "They got dressed and sneaked out. I could see they were trying not to wake me. After they left, I decided to follow them."

She grabbed Corky's arm. "What's going on? *Tell* me!"

"We don't know!" Corky replied.

"We really don't!" Kimmy said. "Ivy sneaked out too. The three of them met up with the basketball players. All of them. It's like they had it all planned or something."

"Well, why weren't *we* invited?" Debra demanded.

Corky shrugged. "We don't know." She pointed to the dark trees. "They all walked off that way." She pointed.

"There's a lake down there. Do you think that's where they're heading?" Debra asked.

"Maybe. Who knows? It's just so weird," Corky replied.

"Come on. We *have* to follow them," Kimmy urged.

Debra turned to Corky. "Was Alex with them?"

Corky nodded. "Yeah. He was there. Jay too. The whole team."

"And Alex didn't tell you anything about a late-night party at the lake? He didn't invite you?" Debra asked.

"No," Corky replied quietly. "He never said a word about it."

"Let's go," Kimmy urged. "If they get too far ahead, we'll lose them."

Debra shivered. "It's so cold."

"Come on," Corky said, making her way across the lot. "It'll be warmer if we move."

A low concrete divider separated the parking lot from the woods. Corky and her friends stepped over it and began to follow a narrow, winding dirt path through the trees.

Their shoes scuffed softly on the hard ground. Pale light from a half moon filtered down through the bare trees, lighting the carpet of dead leaves at their feet.

Nothing is moving, Corky realized, pushing a tall clump of dead weeds out of her way. Not a branch. Not a twig. So eerily still. As if the trees are frozen in place.

To their left, Corky could see the dark outline of the tall cliffs that rose up over the water. The dirt path curved in the other direction, leading them down to the lake.

"Stay back in the trees," Debra warned. "Don't let them see us."

"If they're having a party, we should crash it!" Kimmy declared.

Something scampered through the dead leaves near Corky's feet. Startled, she stumbled. She grabbed on to a slender tree trunk to steady herself.

"What was that?" she managed to cry out, holding a hand over her pounding heart.

"Probably a chipmunk or a field mouse or something," Debra replied. "We *are* out in the woods, you know!"

"We should go back to bed," Corky muttered. "This is crazy! If the others all want to freeze to death, I don't see why we . . ." Her voice trailed off as the lake came into view up ahead.

Through the trees, she saw Lauren and Jay on the frozen water. They were moving in slow motion, dipping their heads and raising their arms awkwardly.

Corky took a few steps closer, staying in the darkness of the woods. Alex and Gary Brandt and Heather also moved in slow motion, side by side, holding hands, raising and lowering their arms as they moved.

They were all out on the lake, Corky saw. They were forming a circle. Their knees bent and their feet sliding slowly over the ice.

The moonlight washed over them, making their faces pale, making their blue shadows tilt and bend over the ice.

And their eyes! Corky felt fear stab her chest as she noticed their eyes. So wide, so vacant. Empty eyes. Unblinking. Staring unfocused like the glass eyes on dolls.

Around and around they danced in slow motion, their heads tilting one way, then another. They held hands and were facing out now, not looking at one another but moving in strange slow unison, as if all part of a single machine.

"What are they doing? What is that dance?" Kimmy whispered, bringing her face so close to Corky that she could feel the warmth of Kimmy's breath on the side of her face.

Debra stirred beside them. Her eyes fixed coldly on the dancing figures, dancing so slowly, so robotlike, in complete silence.

The only sound, Corky realized, was that of the soft shuffle of shoes over ice.

Scrape. Scrape. Scrape.

"What are they *doing?*" Kimmy repeated shrilly.

"Don't you know?" Debra murmured in a low, cold voice. "Don't you see what has happened?"

Alex danced by, staring wide-eyed out at the trees, his expression a blank. He danced between Lauren and Jay, grasped their hands in his, raised them high as he moved in the tight, silent circle.

Heather moved past, dancing between two other players, her coat open, her hair wild about her face, her head tilting from side to side, in perfect unison with the others.

Their shadows dipped and turned, dark blue against the gray ice. Slowly, the dancers moved, as silent as shadows.

And watching them, Corky suddenly knew what was going on.

She understood the dance. Understood their vacant gazes. Understood it all.

She turned to her two friends. And the expressions of horror locked on their faces revealed that they understood too.

"The skating party," Corky murmured.

Debra nodded solemnly. Kimmy let out a low cry.

"Remember? When we called up the spirit?" Corky continued in a trembling voice. "When we accidentally called up the evil from the river bottom?"

"We were pushed back," Kimmy remembered, pressing her hands against her cheeks. "The three of us—we were knocked back over the ice, out of the way."

"But the black smoke poured over them," Debra continued, returning her eyes to the dancing figures on the lake. "We watched it. We watched it rise up from the river and pour out over the cheerleaders and the basketball players. And now—"

Debra stopped. Her expression changed as she squinted toward the lake.

Ferocious growls had broken the eerie silence.

Animal growls.

The dance ended. The circle of dancers broke apart.

The angry snarling grew louder. Closer.

And Corky saw an enormous black dog lumber onto the ice. Glaring at the dancers, it pulled back its lips, revealing a mouthful of long, sharp teeth. Its tail rose stiffly behind it.

The dog uttered a furious howl. Then it tensed its entire body, preparing to attack.

Without realizing it, Corky and her two friends drew closer, eager to see. "See?" Debra whispered. "The dog senses it. The dog senses that they're evil! That's why it's attacking."

The teens on the ice remained silent. They stared back at the raging dog with blank eyes, their faces as devoid of expression as during the slow dance.

No one retreated. No one took a step back.

The dog arched its back. Its black fur on end. It let out a snarl of fury. White spittle poured from its mouth as its jaws flew open.

It leaned back, preparing to pounce.

Suddenly, without signaling to each other, Jay and Ivy stepped forward.

As the ferocious dog leapt to attack, they caught it in midair. Jay grabbed the snarling dog's front legs. Ivy wrapped her hands around the dog's lower trunk.

The dog's head snapped back. Frantically, it jabbed its snout forward, tried to clamp its teeth on Ivy's arm. But the animal wasn't quick enough.

Ivy and Jay heaved it up, straight up.

Corky gasped as the dog sailed high into the air. Higher than the dark trees on the shore.

Higher than any human could throw an enormous dog.

The animal disappeared against the blackness of the sky.

Then it came sailing back down onto the hard ice with a sickening *crack.*

The dazed creature uttered a weak cry. Hobbled to its legs and limped off the ice, its head lowered, tail tucked between its legs, whimpering as it dragged its bruised body away.

Jay and Ivy smiled at each other, a smile of triumph. The others watched without any emotion at all as the dog limped to the trees.

The animal's low whimpers still floated on the air as the teens joined hands and began their dance again. Corky watched the circle of familiar faces, suddenly so unfamiliar, so strange.

So evil.

"They're *all* possessed by the evil," she whispered to Kimmy and Debra.

Debra nodded grimly, her eyes on the silent dancers. "Yes. It's inside every one of them," she murmured with a shudder. "Every one of them."

"What are we going to *do?*" Kimmy demanded shrilly.

Corky replied with a low moan. She gaped in horror at the circle of dancers.

"Corky?" Kimmy cried. "Corky?"

But Corky didn't answer.

She was staring straight ahead at the dancers. The dancers, who had suddenly stopped.

"They—they see us!" Corky stammered. "They're coming for us!"

PART THREE

GOOD-BYE
TIME

Chapter 24

AN INVITATION FROM ALEX

Corky watched as all the vacant sets of eyes turned to her. Watched the circle break. The hands let go. The dancers stopped their slow-motion movements—and started walking slowly, steadily, across the ice to Kimmy, Debra, and her.

As they walked, they bent their heads back and opened their mouths to join in a single shrill wail. An inhuman wail. A terrifying howl of warning.

"Run!" Corky choked out.

She turned and saw Debra making her way through the trees, ducking under low branches, frantically shoving shrubs and brambles away with both hands.

Off to her side, she saw Kimmy slip and fall.

Corky leaned forward and ran along the path, her heart pounding. She could feel the vacant, evil eyes on her back as she forced herself forward through the tangle of brambles and trees.

Kimmy scrambled to her feet and started to run, her eyes wild with fright, her hands outstretched as if reaching for safety.

The evil howl rose through the woods. Like the howl of a hungry wolf.

The sound grew sharper, closer, louder—until Corky was forced to clamp her hands over her ears while she ran.

She saw Debra up ahead, ducking low, dodging the tangle of dark shrubs and weeds. And then she lost her. Couldn't see her anymore. Couldn't hear her shoes on the hard ground.

All she could hear was the wail, the animal wail, the wail of evil.

Gasping for breath, Corky ran. A twig scraped her cheek. Her shoe sank into something soft and mushy. But she didn't slow.

Beyond the trees, the parking lot came into focus, and beyond that, the back of the motel. A sharp pain stabbed her side. She glanced all around. Debra? Kimmy?

She couldn't see them.

But she could hear the sirenlike howl, hear the footsteps of the possessed teens nearing the edge of the woods.

Her shoes scuffed loudly against the asphalt of the

parking lot. The pain in her side grew sharper, made her cry out.

The police! I've got to phone the police! she told herself.

The motel office lights were out. Corky burst up to the door, grabbed the knob. Pulled. Pulled harder.

Locked.

Closed and locked.

Got to call the police!

She sucked in a deep breath of frozen air. Even though the air was cold, her lungs burned. Turning away from the office, she began to jog around the side of the building.

To the front. To the highway.

I'll flag down a car. A passing truck. I'll tell them my friends and I need help. I'll tell them we need the police.

Holding her side, the evil howling still swirling in her ears, Corky made her way to the front. Stepped into the blur of pink and blue neon light. Looked to the highway.

Black and silent.

No cars or trucks.

"Oh!" With a frantic cry, she turned—and saw the glass phone booth on the corner of the lot.

Yes!

Ignoring the pain in her side and the burning in her lungs, she dove forward, grabbed the glass door, pushed it in. Fell into the phone booth. Leaned heavily on the glass as she lifted the receiver.

I don't have a quarter!

Trying to clear her mind. Trying to think with the howls rising all around her, with her heart thumping almost as loudly as the howls.

I don't need a quarter to call the police.

All I have to do is—

She lifted the receiver to her ear.

Silence.

She pushed O.

Silence.

She pushed 911.

Silence.

It's broken, she realized. The phone is dead.

Dead.

I'll be dead, unless I can get away. . . .

She turned and pulled in the glass door to make her escape—and found Alex blocking her way.

He grinned at her, his blue eyes burning into hers. His blond hair, unbrushed as always, fell over his forehead. He was breathing heavily, his chest heaving under his bulky gray sweater.

"Alex—let me go!" Corky shrieked, desperately tugging at the door.

But he raised his hands on the frame of the booth and stood in her path, blocking the door with his body.

"Alex—please!" she begged.

His eyes narrowed sympathetically at her, crinkling.

I used to find that so cute, so attractive, Corky

thought, gasping for breath, staring back at him in horror.

"Corky, what's wrong?" Alex asked softly.

"Just let me go!" she pleaded, trying to shove him out of the way with both hands.

He didn't budge. "What's wrong?" he repeated innocently. "Why did you run away?"

"Alex—I—I—"

He reached into the phone booth and grabbed her hand. Her hand was cold. His was hot, burning hot. "Corky, come to the lake with us." He tried to tug her from the booth.

"No, Alex. No, I won't!" Corky cried, trembling all over.

"Yes, you will," Alex insisted softly, still smiling, ignoring her terror. "Come to the lake. Come now, Corky. We'll have so much fun. You'll see."

Chapter 25

KIMMY ON ICE

"No, Alex—please!"

Corky tried to pull free. But he held on to her hand with inhuman strength.

"Alex—let *go!*"

He didn't seem to hear her. His smile remained set. His eyes bored into hers, cold and uncaring.

With a hard jerk of his hand, he tugged her from the phone booth. Corky cried out. Swung her fist. Her punch glanced off his shoulder.

She punched him again. His smile widened.

"Come to the lake, Corky," he urged softly. "Come have fun with us."

This isn't Alex, Corky told herself, staring at his

grinning face in horror. This isn't the real Alex, the Alex that I knew, that I cared about.

This is a different Alex, inhabited by the evil. He doesn't even know he's doing this. He doesn't even know he's dragging me back to the lake—probably to kill me.

He gripped her wrists with both hands now and began to pull her toward the back of the motel, toward the woods.

Her eyes searched the parking lot frantically. Where are Kimmy and Debra? Corky wondered. Did they get away?

Where are the rest of the cheerleaders and basketball players? Did they go back to the lake? Are they all waiting for me there?

A truck roared by on the highway. Corky opened her mouth to call for help. But it sped past before she could get out a sound.

"Come to the lake, Corky. You and I always have fun—don't we?" Alex whispered, his breath hot against her face.

What if I scream? she asked herself as he dragged her into the woods. Will someone in the motel wake up? Will they come hurrying out to help me?

The rooms were all dark. There was only the black Jeep in the lot in back.

It's worth a try, Corky thought.

As if reading her thoughts, Alex clamped a hand tightly over her mouth. Corky's cry was smothered.

With a burst of rage, she dropped low. Spun free. Scrambled forward.

Into the trees. On all fours for a few seconds. Then up. Onto her feet. Leaning forward. Keeping herself low.

Through some low scrub, branches cutting at her legs right through her jeans. Stumbling over a fallen tree trunk. Gaining her balance. Struggling forward.

"Hey!" Alex, startled, calling after her from close behind. "Hey! Hey, Corky!"

Scrambling away from him, she slid over dead leaves. The morning sun, just poking over the horizon, cast a wash of purple over everything, making the woods appear dreamlike, unreal.

"Hey, Corky! Hey!"

His voice farther behind her now. Off to the left.

Had he lost her? Had she confused him?

She didn't have time to think, to figure out where to run.

She realized she was heading back toward the lake, but Corky didn't care. She was getting away.

For now.

Oh! She forced herself not to cry out as a slender, low branch slapped her face. She could feel the sting of it on her cheek as she kept running, weaving, crisscrossing behind shrubs and trees, trying to leave Alex behind.

Kimmy, where are you? she wondered, her eyes struggling to focus through the haze of purple. Debra —you were ahead of me. Did you get away?

She had a sudden urge to call to her friends. But she realized that would only allow Alex to find her, to capture her again.

The lake stretched just ahead, the ice a blue-purple under the low morning sun. Corky stopped, panting loudly.

No one there.

No one on the lake.

Where had they gone? Had they returned to the motel? Were they somewhere in the woods chasing Debra and Kimmy?

We know their secret, Corky thought, feeling a fresh chill run down her back, Kimmy, Debra, and I—we know the secret of their evil.

That is why they came after us.

That is why they will not let us escape alive.

She heard a scrabbling in the bushes behind her. Alex?

Yes. She heard his muttered curses. Then she heard him change his tone and call to her again: "Corky? Come here, Corky. It's me—Alex! Don't be afraid of me! I want to help you!"

No, you don't, Corky thought bitterly. You don't want to help me, Alex. You want to *hurt* me.

Her eyes searched the frozen shore for a hiding place.

Where can I go?

She saw a shrub move just behind the nearest trees. Alex was getting closer. Soon he would see her. Soon he would catch her.

Struggling to think clearly, struggling to find a path of escape, Corky backed up. One step, another.

I've got to get away from him. Got to get to a hiding place.

She raised her hands to her face and kept her eyes forward as she backed up.

Where can I go?

"Hey!" She cried out as her feet started to slide out from under her. Without realizing it, she had backed onto the frozen surface of the lake.

She barely got her balance.

She glanced down.

"NOOOO!" Her scream echoed off the bare trees.

Two eyes stared up at her from under the ice. Two lifeless eyes. Black hair floated around the face, billowing in the frozen water beneath the ice.

Pain made Corky drop to her knees. She felt as if someone had punched her in the stomach. She bent over the face staring up at her, the dead, bloated face under the ice.

Kimmy's face.

Corky forgot about Alex, lifted her eyes from the horrifying sight, and let out a furious howl of rage.

Chapter 26

ANOTHER CORPSE

On her hands and knees on the ice, Corky stared down at her friend. Kimmy's face pushed up against the surface, her hair billowing out like dark seaweed.

They drowned her, Corky realized, her entire body trembling. They trapped Kimmy under the ice and drowned her because she knew the truth about them.

Corky couldn't take her eyes off the pale, watery face that stared up at her. Did they drown Debra too? she wondered, unable to stop her trembling.

Hot tears rolled down her cheeks. As they hit the frozen surface, they sent up tiny puffs of steam.

They'll drown me next, Corky realized.

They'll catch me and force me under, trap me under the ice and watch me drown.

She forced herself to her knees, wiping the tears from her cheeks with both hands. I've got to stop them, she told herself. I've got to find a way to stop them.

And I have to pay them back for murdering poor Kimmy.

Once again she pictured Alex's smile, his inviting eyes pleading with her to come to the lake. He's evil, she knew. They're all evil. They're not the kids I knew.

They drowned Kimmy.

They want to drown me.

A rustling in the woods made her turn away. She saw tall weeds bend. Heard the soft swish of footsteps on wet leaves.

They're coming for me. Got to get away. Got to run.

Without realizing it, she had climbed to her feet. Now she was making her way back into the woods, stumbling, staggering, lurching unsteadily. Her legs felt as if they were made of stone. She forced them forward, forced them to move, one step, then another.

The morning sun had risen above the treetops, casting golden light that trickled down through the trees. The bare branches reached out for Corky as she hurtled between trees that were deliberately blocking her path.

Turning back, she raised her eyes to the tall purple cliffs that overlooked the lake. I should've run in that direction, she thought. I could've climbed the cliffs and escaped.

Corky saw two figures move out onto the frozen

lake. She recognized Jay, his Mighty Ducks cap on backward, his hands shoved into the pockets of his Shadyside High jacket. He was spinning slowly, his eyes searching the shore.

Searching for me, Corky realized with a shudder.

Through the tangle of tree branches, Corky could see Lauren step up beside him. Lauren shielded her eyes with one hand as she searched the woods for Corky.

They used to be my friends, Corky thought, turning away. Jay always made me laugh.

Now he wants to kill me.

"There she is!" she heard Lauren cry.

Corky froze at the sound. Her entire body suddenly felt as cold as the ice on the lake.

With a low cry, she willed her legs to move. But they wouldn't cooperate.

Ice. I've turned to ice, she thought.

She heard the crackle of dead leaves, rapid footsteps as Jay and Lauren hurried to capture her.

Corky sucked in a deep chestful of cold air. Got to move. Got to move! she urged herself.

"Corky—where are you?" Alex's voice. Nearby.

They're circling me. They're trapping me.

No!

With a surge of effort, she bolted forward. Grabbing a tree trunk, she hurtled herself deeper into the woods.

"Corky—I want to talk to you!" Alex's phony pleading from somewhere to her left. "I just want to talk, Corky!"

She cut sharply to the right. Felt the prickle of burrs against her cheek. Brushed them away and, ducking her head, kept moving.

Deeper into the woods.

The voices followed her, voices she knew so well, the voices of strangers now.

"Where is she?"

"I just saw her."

"We have to form a wider circle. All of us. Then just tighten it around her."

"We may be too late. She may be on her way back to the motel."

"She won't get away. If she comes out of the woods, we'll have her."

Corky forced back a sob. Her chest felt ready to burst.

The voices were so close!

Dark trees circled her, appeared to be closing in. She spotted a double trunk, two trees growing together, entwined as one. With a desperate lunge, Corky darted behind the wide trunk, slid into the coolness of the indentation between the two trunks.

Waited. And listened hard, trying to slow the pounding of her heart.

The crunch of footsteps grew louder. The voices nearer.

"Corky? It's me, Alex. Corky? Where are you?"

"Corky? The bus is waiting. It's time to go to the arena." Heather's voice, so close. Was she standing right in front of the double tree trunk?

Holding her breath, Corky sank back against the smooth bark. She shut her eyes and prayed, willing them away.

Go. Please go. Go search somewhere else.

She heard the crackle of leaves. Heard the sharp crack of a twig breaking. Heard their muttered curses as they continued to search.

"Corky—it's Lauren! Ms. Closter wants to see you back at the motel!"

"Hey, Corky—what's the problem?" Jay's voice, somewhere to her left. "Why are you hiding from your friends?"

And then Heather's voice again. "Corky—it's time to go to the game!"

Go. Please go. Please please *please!*

Corky's entire body tensed, every muscle tightened as she prayed for them to leave.

A few seconds passed. Then a few more.

A bird whistled loudly above her head. A shrill whistle, like a warning call. Corky raised her eyes and saw a large bluejay perched above her on a high limb.

A few seconds later she heard the flutter of wings. A shadow rolled over her as the jay took flight.

And then the woods lay silent.

Pressing her back against the hard trunk, Corky held her breath and listened. No footsteps. No voices.

A soft wind off the lake made the bare tree limbs rattle and creak.

She heard a soft *thud.* A nest off a tree limb?

Then only silence.

Is it a trap? Corky wondered, still gripped with fear. Are they waiting on the other side of this tree, waiting to pounce?

Have they left? Or are they all standing there, watching the tree trunk, watching for me to show myself?

The silence grew heavy. Corky's ears rang.

She had to find out.

She had to know.

Taking a deep breath, Corky kept her back to the tree trunk as she edged to the side—and peeked out.

She gasped in surprise when she saw the lifeless body lying on the ground.

Chapter 27

EVERYBODY DROWNS

Corky stared down in shock at the dead bluejay.

Why did they have to kill it? she wondered.

Just because they could?

Its wings spread against the ground, its feet poking straight up in the air, the bird's head tilted at an unnatural angle. One lifeless black eye stared accusingly at Corky.

They will kill everything, she thought. Everyone and everything.

Her eyes darted, making a wide circle of the woods.

No one there. They really had moved their search to another part of the woods.

With a sigh, Corky dropped down heavily onto a

fallen tree trunk and buried her head in her hands. Her entire body convulsed in a sharp tremor of terror. She realized she had never been this frightened in her entire life.

They were gone for now. But they'd be back.

She had to get away, away from the lake and these woods, away from the town. Away.

She had to get help. She had to find a way to stop them.

But right now, she realized, she couldn't move from the fallen tree. Couldn't raise her head from her hands. Couldn't stop her body from trembling.

Paralyzed by her fear, Corky lost track of time.

Had a few seconds passed? Minutes? An hour or two?

The sun's warmth on the back of her head brought her back to full consciousness. She stood up, tossing back her hair, blinking at the bright golden sunlight. The few patches of still white snow glistened as if dotted with a million tiny diamonds.

Corky stretched, raising her hands high above her head, arching her back. Then she started to jog, pushing shrubs out of her way with both hands.

I'll get to the highway and just keep running till a car stops for me or I find a phone, she decided.

But she stopped at the edge of the motel parking lot when she saw the yellow bus. The gray-uniformed driver stood beside the open door as Heather and Lauren, in their cheerleader uniforms, climbed on.

Gary and Jay were shoving each other playfully,

bumping shoulders, laughing as they stumbled through the door.

They're going to the arena for our next game, Corky realized, taking a step closer. She made her way onto the parking lot and ducked low behind a maroon minivan.

Peering out from in front of the hood, Corky saw that on the bus were the Shadyside players and cheerleaders. The driver must have picked up the boys first. Through the windows she could see them laughing and talking excitedly.

As if nothing had happened. As if everything were normal.

As if Kimmy weren't frozen beneath the ice in the lake.

Swallowing hard, Corky searched each window for Debra. But didn't see her.

Doesn't anyone wonder where Kimmy and Debra and I are? Corky wondered.

She quickly answered her own question: No. Of course not. They *know* where we are. They *know* everything isn't normal. They're all putting on an act.

They're having a wonderful time, she thought bitterly. Look at them, laughing and joking with one another!

The sight forced a sob from Corky's throat. She felt all her muscles tighten as a wave of fury swept over her body.

The bus driver climbed onto the bus. A few seconds later, the door closed. The engine sputtered to life.

Corky stepped away from the minivan, her eyes on the smiling faces inside the bus. She wanted to scream. She wanted to throw herself in front of the bus. To stop them. To stop their laughter, their jokes.

To her surprise, the bus door swung open. The driver climbed down. Shaking his head, he made his way toward the motel office, taking long, rapid strides.

He must have left something there, Corky thought. Or maybe he has to make a call.

A sudden flash of inspiration made Corky move quickly.

The idea swept into her mind, fueled by her frustration, her bitter anger.

Staying low behind the parked cars, she hurtled herself toward the bus. Then, gasping in a deep breath and holding it, she grabbed the sides of the bus doorway, pushed herself up the steps, and dove into the driver's seat.

Had anyone seen her?

Corky let out her breath in a loud *whoosh* and listened.

No. The laughing and excited conversations continued without interruption. No one called her name or shouted out to her.

She glanced in the wide rearview mirror. She saw Jay and Alex near the back, slapping each other a high-five, laughing gleefully. She turned the mirror until she couldn't see anyone. Now no one could see her.

Corky slammed the door shut.

A solid partition closed her off from the rest of the bus and hid her. She released the emergency brake and slid both hands around the big steering wheel.

Slipping the bus into gear, Corky leaned forward and lowered her foot on the large gas pedal. Corky pressed harder on the gas, and the bus rumbled out of the parking lot, bumped over a curb, and onto the highway. Behind her, Corky heard kids laugh and cheer as the bus hit the bump and bounced hard.

Leaning over the wheel, Corky listened to their conversations. They hadn't heard the driver shout at the bus.

And none of them seemed to realize that the bus was heading *away* from the New Foster Arena.

Behind her, loud cheers erupted as the bus bounced into a deep pothole. Without slowing, Corky turned off the highway and onto a narrow road called Cliffview.

She didn't know the town or the roads. But she took a guess that the road had to lead to where she wanted to go. As the road curved up through the thick woods, Corky wondered if she'd made the right choice.

I can't really do this—can I? she asked herself.

She began to feel more doubts. She lightened her foot on the gas pedal.

I can't do this. It seemed like a good plan—the only plan. But I can't carry it out.

Kimmy's face forced her forward.

The big steering wheel bounced under her hands as Corky pressed all the way down on the gas. The bus

177

rumbled and roared, tires spinning on the slick, icy surface as it climbed higher through the glistening woods.

Her features set, her eyes staring straight ahead, Corky pictured Kimmy's eyes peering up so blankly, so sadly at her from under the frozen lake. She saw Kimmy's black hair billowing in the water.

And she pictured Kimmy's mouth, the lips opening slowly, forming the words, "Keep going."

"Keep going."

The bloated purple lips. The eyes pleading.

"Keep going."

Corky imagined Kimmy's last request. Poor, drowned Kimmy. Kimmy under the ice in her watery grave. Drowned by the evil. Drowned by the evil on board this bus.

Kimmy's face, so clear in Corky's mind, urged Corky forward.

Stayed with her. Rode with her.

Kimmy is here with me, Corky thought. Sitting beside me, guiding me. Telling me that what I am about to do is right. Telling me that I have no choice.

Corky realized that she was doing the only thing she could. These weren't really her friends. They were the evil. Corky knew that she had to drown the evil— push it out of her friends' bodies. It was their only chance of survival. If she didn't drown the evil, her friends would die for sure.

Corky could only hope that—once the evil had left them—her friends would survive. Just as she had when she forced the evil from her own body.

Gripping the wheel tightly in both hands, Corky leaned over it, staring out the windshield, watching the blur of trees bounce past.

She slowed as the cliff edge came into view.

A low metal railing had been placed along the side of the road. It was more of a warning than a fence, Corky thought. A warning that the ground ended sharply in a steep drop, a steep drop all the way down to the frozen lake.

The low divider wouldn't stop a car from plunging over the side.

Or a bus.

She grabbed the door control. The bus bounced near the low metal railing. Then back to the center of the road.

Peering down, Corky saw the lake far below. It gleamed under the late-morning sun like a vast shiny mirror.

"Corky? Corky, what are you doing?"

Corky heard a voice call out behind her. Someone had recognized her. Too late. Nothing could stop her now. She had to go through with her plan. It was the only chance she had of saving her friends.

"Ohhhh." A frightened moan escaped her throat.

Am I doing this?

Am I?

Kimmy's dead face appealed to her one last time: "Keep going."

Corky eased her foot down on the brake. Slowed the bus.

Slower. Slower.

179

She opened the bus door.

Slower. Slower.

Can I do it? Can I do it now?

Yes!

She turned the wheel hard toward the cliff edge. Then, holding the wheel with one hand, Corky pushed herself up from the seat, ran to the open doorway—and jumped.

She hit the pavement hard, landing on her right shoulder. Then she rolled into the metal railing. It clanged loudly, and held her.

Ignoring the pain that shot out from her shoulder, Corky pulled herself to a sitting position—in time to see the yellow bus plunge through the divider and over the cliff.

Raising her hands to her face, she watched it tilt straight down and then plummet out of view, its tires spinning in air.

She heard the terrified squeals and shrieks of the players and three cheerleaders. The cries ended in a loud *crack* and then *splash* that brought Corky to her feet.

Peering over the side of the cliff, Corky saw the rear of the bus sticking straight up, sinking rapidly into a wide blue pool of water.

Silvery sheets of ice had been split away by the impact. The ice sheets bobbed and tilted over the water like fallen walls of a house. The bus dropped between them.

In the distance Corky saw several men in parkas out on the ice. Ice fishermen. They dropped their poles and shouted. Running over the ice toward the sinking bus.

Too late.

A large air bubble rose up in the blue water as the back of the bus sank below the surface.

The screams and shrieks vanished. Cut off, like someone clicking off a radio.

The only sounds now were the rough scraping of the broken ice sheets as they splashed against one another and the distressed cries of the ice fishermen.

Sobbing loudly, both hands still pressed against her cheeks, Corky stared down into the blue hole in the ice. She watched as the water started to bubble and boil. Watched as the thick steam poured up from the hole.

Corky knew that this was the evil drowning. Being forced from her friends' bodies.

Corky watched as the steam continued to billow up from the ice.

No one came up.

No one swam to the surface.

Corky drowned the evil.

But had she drowned all her friends too?

Chapter 28

TEAM SPIRIT

The evil had to be drowned, Corky knew. Drowning was the only way to defeat it.

But as she stared down over the cliff edge, Corky felt no relief. She felt only sorrow and fear.

I've drowned everyone, she realized with a shock. I've killed all my friends.

Staggering away from the guardrail, she made her way unsteadily down the hill to the highway. The road, the trees, all blurred before her. As she stepped onto the highway, it appeared to buckle and bend beneath her feet.

The ground tilted hard to the right, then swayed to the left. Dizzy, afraid she'd fall, Corky grabbed hold of a telephone pole.

Wrapping one arm around the pole, she shut her eyes. Even with her eyes shut, the world continued to spin.

What is happening to me? she wondered.

Then another frightening question forced itself into her mind. What *will* happen to me? What will happen when they find out I drowned all my friends?

She shook her head, forcing the question away. Then she pushed herself from the pole.

Go to the arena, she instructed herself. Tell them what has happened. Tell Ms. Closter. Tell everyone.

The team is dead. The cheerleaders are dead.

I sent them over the cliff. I drowned them all. Because I had to drown the evil.

"Got to tell," Corky murmured, stumbling along the shoulder. She slipped on a patch of ice. "Got to tell. Got to tell everything."

Dragging herself along the highway, murmuring to herself, Corky ignored the swaying, tilting ground, ignored the bright blur of the woods. Dazed, she walked blindly toward the arena.

Cars and trucks whirred by. Part of the blur of color that danced before her eyes.

After she had walked half an hour, a station wagon slowed to a stop. A boy leaned out the passenger window and called to her, "Going to the game? Want a ride?"

When Corky didn't reply, the station wagon sped off.

"Got to explain," she repeated over and over as she

continued her slow, unsteady journey. "Got to tell. Got to tell everything."

The sun beamed down, but didn't warm her. Shivering, dazed, muttering to herself, she lost all track of time. When the arena came into view, Corky nearly walked past it.

The excited shouts of people making their way into the entrances snapped Corky out of her haze. She followed the lines into the brightly lit arena.

"Got to tell. Got to tell."

"Ticket, miss?" A hand thrust itself in her face.

"Huh?" She stared at a tall man in a red blazer.

"Ticket. I need to see your ticket," he said patiently.

"Oh. I'm a cheerleader," Corky told him, struggling to see past him down the long aisle to the basketball floor.

"You're a cheerleader? Where's your uniform?" the man asked, frowning.

"Back at the motel," Corky answered absently.

"Miss, I can't let you in unless—"

"But I've got to tell! Got to tell!" she cried. And plunged past him, past his outstretched hand, into the arena, her shoes clomping on the concrete steps.

Faces. Faces all around her. People in the stands.

And down on the floor she saw a team warming up. Their uniforms white.

Only one team warming up, taking practice shots. Only one team—and Corky knew why.

"Ms. Closter!" she called, her voice shrill and strange to herself. "Ms. Closter! It's me!"

She saw the coach across the floor, her arms crossed

over the front of her white T-shirt, talking calmly to a referee.

"Ms. Closter! Please!"

Ms. Closter glanced up at the sound of Corky's frantic cry.

Corky breathlessly ran across the middle of the basketball court, ignoring the startled cries of the players.

"Corky—everyone is late!" Ms. Closter said, frowning. "Do you know where the bus is?"

"In the lake," Corky told her. Everything spun around her. The rows of seats, the two backboards, the empty team benches. She thought she saw Debra, but it was so hard to tell. Everything was spinning. Spinning so rapidly.

"The game has to be canceled!" she shrieked, tearing at her hair with both hands, trying to make it all stop spinning.

"Huh?" Ms. Closter's eyes narrowed.

"They're all dead!" Corky screamed. "All dead!"

But her horrifying words were drowned out by a loud cheer that roared down from the stands.

A band started playing. The cheering rose over the blaring brass.

"I can't hear you!" Ms. Closter cried, cupping both ears and leaning close to Corky. "What did you say?"

"I said they're all dead!" Corky choked out.

Ms. Closter shook her head. "Sorry. It's so noisy—"

Corky took a deep breath. She opened her mouth to shout again.

The roar of the crowd made her turn her head.

She saw a team make its way onto the floor.

Team? What team? she wondered, struggling to focus.

The band played enthusiastically as the players moved under the bright lights.

Corky gasped as she recognized them. Alex. And Jay. Gary. The other Shadyside players.

Too stunned to cry out, she watched Ivy, Heather, and Lauren follow the team onto the floor, jumping and clapping.

"No! No!" Corky shouted out loud.

The band music sputtered out abruptly. And the cheers of the crowd turned to horrified, sickened groans.

Their faces! Corky saw. The players' faces. They were wet, and puffy, and bloated. Clumps of green lake moss clung to their hair. Wet mud ran down their cheeks and stained their uniforms.

Corky gaped in openmouthed shock at their frightening, dead faces. At their vacant eyes, empty, lifeless eyes.

The players tried to pick up basketballs to begin their warm-ups. But the balls fell heavily from their limp, water-bloated hands.

"No! No! No!" Corky repeated her horrified chant as the three cheerleaders lined up and started a cheer. Their uniforms were soaked and stained. Clumps of mud and dead leaves fell from their hair as they jumped.

Brackish brown water poured out of their open

mouths and dribbled down their chins. They moved their swollen lips silently, spewing a steady stream of murky water.

More groans rose up from the crowd. Children were crying. Terrified screams echoed off the high walls.

"They're dead! They're dead!" Corky shouted.

And as she shouted, Alex turned to her. His dead eyes glowed at her from across the floor. He had a deep purple gash down the side of his face, but no blood spilled from it. Alex lurched clumsily to Jay and pointed a swollen finger at Corky.

An eerie grin crossed Jay's fat, purple lips as he staggered over to Alex. One of his eyes had sunken back in its socket. The other squinted at Corky.

"They're dead! They're all dead!" Corky, dazed and dizzy, continued to chant.

She stopped her cries, and her breath caught in her throat when she realized they were all staring at her now. The dead players and the three dead cheerleaders.

All staring at her with their blank eyes.

And now, all staggering toward her, lurching, stumbling after her, reaching for her with their swollen purple hands, coming for her, coming for their revenge.

Chapter 29

"THE GANG'S ALL HERE"

As a wave of terror swept over her, Corky stumbled back against the bench.

Alex, Jay, and the others staggered toward her. Jay had a broken arm, Corky saw. It hung loosely at his side. A pale white bone poked out through the skin at his elbow.

Her streaked hair wet and matted, Ivy grinned at Corky. All her teeth had been knocked out. Dark bloodstains caked her chin.

Gary's head twitched violently, bobbing from side to side on his broken neck as he moved with the others. A reeling, lurching line closed in on Corky.

She stared in horror from face to face. They're all dead, she realized. They're the walking dead!

Corky wanted to back away. But the bench blocked her way.

She spun around—her heart banging, her temples throbbing, so dizzy and dazed—and saw people frantically jamming the aisles, desperate to flee the arena.

Frightened shrieks and cries rang out through the vast building. And over the moans and shouts she heard a shrill voice calling her name. *"Corky! Corky!"*

Corky gasped when she saw Debra, her blond hair tangled about her head, her blue eyes wild, charging across the floor to her. "Oh, no, Debra!" Corky cried out loud. "They got you too? They got you too?"

And then the bloated bodies blocked out all the light. And hands reached for Corky. The swollen, broken fingers grasped for her throat.

She felt the icy, wet touch of death wrap itself around her.

And a heavy darkness swept her down, down to the floor.

When she opened her eyes, she saw only white. She blinked. Once. Twice. But she couldn't bring anything into focus.

I'm dead, Corky thought.

This is what death looks like. A wall of white surrounded by white.

She felt a dull ache at the back of her head.

How did I die? she wondered, struggling to remember. But her mind seemed as blank as the solid wash of white around her.

Groaning from the pain, she pulled herself up. Realized she was in a bed. In a room.

An open doorway came into focus.

Corky heard voices on the other side of the doorway. She took a deep breath. A strong aroma invaded her nose. Disinfectant? Rubbing alcohol?

The dull pain throbbed. She raised a hand and rubbed the back of her head through her tangled hair.

A young woman with curly red hair appeared in the doorway. Corky stared at her white uniform.

A nurse. I'm not dead, she realized. I'm in a hospital.

"You're up? That's great!" the nurse exclaimed, smiling. She had a high, squeaky voice. "Your parents are on their way."

"My parents?" Corky's mouth felt dry. It was a struggle to get the words out.

"You're going to be okay," the nurse told her, stepping into the room. "You fainted and hit your head. That's what your coach told us. It knocked you out. But there's no internal bleeding or anything. You'll be all right."

Corky stared at her, letting this information sink in. "I'm okay?"

"A pretty bad concussion," the nurse replied, her eyes studying Corky. "Your coach said you acted dazed when you arrived at the arena. And I guess with all the excitement—"

"But—but my friends?" Corky stammered.

"Your friends are all here in the hospital," the nurse

replied casually. A strange smile formed on her full lips. "It's been a busy day."

My friends are all here?

The words sent a frozen chill that shook Corky's body.

My dead friends are all here in the hospital?

They all followed me here, Corky realized.

The nurse is wrong. Everything *isn't* going to be okay.

They're not going to let me leave alive.

Chapter 30

GRABBED

I have to get out of here as fast as I can, Corky realized.

She waited for the nurse to leave. Then she lowered her feet to the floor and stood up. Ignoring her dizziness and the dull pain at the back of her head, Corky spotted her clothes hanging in an open closet against the wall.

With one eye on the door, she tugged off the pale green hospital gown and climbed into her jeans. As she pulled her sweater over her head, she shivered again.

They're here. They're all here, she realized.

Lying in hospital rooms. Waiting to come for me.

The dead players. The dead cheerleaders. All here.

Grabbing her jacket off the hanger, Corky turned and started to the door. I'll find a back exit. I'll run out, she told herself. I'll hide and wait for my parents near the parking lot.

Thinking about her parents gave Corky some hope. I can do it, she told herself. I can get out of here.

She took a step toward the door—and stopped short as a figure appeared, blocking her way.

"Debra!" Corky cried.

Debra wore her maroon and white cheerleader uniform. Her cold blue eyes studied Corky. "You're up?" she demanded.

"Let me go!" Corky shrieked. "Debra—please! Let me go!"

Without waiting for a reply, Corky pushed past Debra, shoving her in the ribs and shooting out the doorway. She heard Debra's cry of surprise behind her. But she didn't glance back.

Corky hurtled down the long hallway, the pale green walls and open doorways whirring past in a blur, her shoes pounding the hard linoleum floor.

"Corky—wait!" Debra's desperate cry behind her.

No. I can't let her catch me. I can't! Corky urged herself forward, ignoring the pain in her head, ignoring the pounding at her temples.

She's dead. Debra is dead. And now she wants to kill *me*.

"Corky—stop!"

Corky tore around a corner, nearly collided with two uniformed nurses pushing a food cart. "Hey!" one of them called sharply.

Were they going to chase her too?

Her heart pounding hard inside her chest, Corky searched for a hiding place. She saw a room filled with visitors.

The next room appeared empty. Corky peered inside. She stopped when she saw the familiar face of the boy in the bed.

Alex.

His eyes closed. His lips slightly parted.

"Corky—come back!"

Debra's frantic cry forced Corky into Alex's room. She stepped in, pulling the door closed behind her.

Alex slept peacefully, she saw.

Poor, dead Alex.

Even though he's dead, the evil won't let him rest long. The evil must still be inside him.

She crept closer to the bed, feeling sad and frightened at the same time.

He breathed softly, steadily. His eyelids fluttered but didn't open.

I'm sorry, Alex, Corky thought, watching him sleep. I'm sorry I had to drown you. I cared about you. I really did.

Alex's right hand shot up from under the sheet.

It grabbed Corky by the wrist.

Corky cried out and struggled to pull free.

But the hand held tight. Pulled her close as Alex opened his eyes, sat up, raised his face to hers—and pressed his mouth against hers.

The kiss of death! Corky thought, struggling to free herself as his dry lips pressed hard against hers.

Chapter 31

DEFEATED

Corky felt a wave of nausea rise from her stomach. I'm kissing a dead boy, she thought. I'm kissing a corpse.

To her surprise, Alex's hand slipped off her wrist. He pulled back and smiled at her. "Corky, I'm so glad you're okay," he declared.

"Huh?" Corky staggered back from his bed, raising a hand to her chest as if to steady her racing heart.

"It was so terrifying," Alex continued, his blue eyes locked on hers. "Like the worst nightmare, only it was really happening. I—I can't describe what it felt like. We all thought we were going to drown."

"Y-you *thought—*" Corky stammered.

"Where were you?" Alex demanded. "How come you weren't on the bus, Corky?"

She stared at him, unable to answer.

He didn't know that she *had* been on the bus. She had been the driver.

"I don't remember much," he said as if reading her thoughts. "I don't remember the bus going over the cliff. I don't really remember sinking under the water. I guess my panic wiped out the memories."

He smiled and shook his head. "If those guys hadn't been ice fishing nearby . . ."

"Ice fishing?" Corky choked out.

"They pulled us out," Alex told her. "They were great. There were only three of them. And they pulled every one of us out of that sunken bus. They saved all our lives!"

Alex sat up, grinning at her. "Look at me! I'm okay! Isn't that amazing?"

"Yes. Amazing," Corky echoed.

His expression changed. "Want to hear something else weird? None of us got frostbite—because the water wasn't cold. It was *hot*, Corky. The water was actually steaming! Isn't that strange?"

"Yes. Strange," she repeated, thinking hard.

The water was hot because the evil was in it, Corky knew. She had drowned the evil after all. Drowned the evil—and then her friends were rescued.

"Alex, I—I'm so glad," Corky stammered, staring hard at him.

He's really normal, she thought happily. He's really Alex.

"But you all came to the arena," Corky blurted out. "You were soaked. And weird. And you staggered into the arena, and—"

Alex's smile faded. "The nurse told me you had a concussion," he said softly. "You must have dreamed that we came to the arena. Or hallucinated it or something. We never made it to the arena. The ice fishermen got us here to the hospital right away."

So the horrifying scene in the arena never happened, Corky realized. It had all been in her head.

I wish I had imagined all the rest, she thought sadly.

"Alex, what about Kimmy?" Corky asked suddenly.

"Oh, Corky," Alex replied. "Kimmy's dead. I don't know how it happened. But by the time they found her body, it was too late. She must have fallen through the ice and drowned."

The door to the room swung open. Debra burst inside. She glanced at Alex, then turned her eyes to Corky. "Corky, why'd you run away from me?" she asked breathlessly.

"I—I thought—" Corky felt too confused to form words. "Debra, you weren't on the bus?" she finally managed to say.

Debra shook her head. "They were chasing us down by the lake, remember?" she replied. "I ran. I was so frightened. I ran to the motel, but I didn't stop. I just kept running. Down the highway. I didn't know where I was going or what I planned to do. I just knew I couldn't stop."

So they didn't catch Debra, Corky realized. Debra didn't die. Only poor Kimmy died.

Poor Kimmy, Corky thought sadly. My poor, lost friend.

Debra got away.

"I hid for a while behind a restaurant," Debra continued. "Then I made my way to the arena. I saw you, Corky, in front of the bench. I was so glad you'd escaped too. I ran to you. But you fainted before I could get to you. I saw you collapse and hit your head."

And that's when I must have dreamed that the dead players and cheerleaders staggered into the arena, Corky realized.

"Oh, I'm so glad you're okay! I'm so glad we're *all* okay!"

"Yeah," said Alex. "I still can't believe everyone survived."

Everyone except Kimmy, Corky thought sadly. She rushed forward and hugged Debra. Then she stepped to the bed and took Alex's hand in hers. His warm hand. His *alive* hand.

Tears rolled down Corky's cheeks. She looked down at Alex. He didn't remember any of it, she realized. He and the others who were possessed by the evil would never remember what they had done.

Corky thought of Lena, the cheerleader who couldn't stop flipping.

At last, her terror would end.

The nightmare was over. The evil was gone.

Corky had drowned it.

She had defeated it.

The evil had died. Corky had lived.

She squeezed Alex's hand. He returned her smile. "Do you realize what today is?" he asked.

"Saturday?" Debra replied.

"No. It's Christmas Eve," Alex told them.

Corky glanced down at her white hospital gown and then at Alex's. She laughed. "I don't think this is what they mean by a white Christmas!" she joked.

"Well, Merry Christmas anyway," Alex declared brightly.

"Merry Christmas to us all!" Corky cried. "Now, when can we all go home?"

About the Author

"Where do you get your ideas?"

That's the question that R. L. Stine is asked most often. "I don't know where my ideas come from," he says. "But I do know that I have a lot more scary stories in my mind that I can't wait to write."

So far, he has written over fifty mysteries and thrillers for young people, all of them bestsellers.

Bob grew up in Columbus, Ohio. Today he lives in an apartment near Central Park in New York City with his wife, Jane, and fourteen-year-old son, Matt.

THE NIGHTMARES
NEVER END . . .
WHEN YOU VISIT

Next . . .
WRONG NUMBER 2
(Coming in January 1995)

It's been over a year since Deena and Jade played any phone pranks. Over a year since the night they called the house on Fear Street—and interrupted a murder. Stanley Farberson killed his wife—then he came after Deena and Jade. But now he's in jail, behind bars. And they're safe. Or are they?

Suddenly, the girls start getting mysterious phone calls. Threatening phone calls, repeating things that only Farberson could know. Deena and Jade are terrified—could it be him? Is their wrong number coming back for revenge?